Twist of Fate

Also from Jill Shalvis

The Heartbreaker Bay series
SWEET LITTLE LIES
THE TROUBLE WITH MISTLETOE
ACCIDENTALLY ON PURPOSE
CHASING CHRISTMAS EVE
ABOUT THAT KISS
HOT WINTER NIGHTS
PLAYING FOR KEEPS
WRAPPED UP IN YOU

The Wildstone series
LOST AND FOUND SISTERS
RAINY DAY FRIENDS
THE LEMON SISTERS
THE GOOD LUCK SISTER

COMING SOON

ALMOST JUST FRIENDS
THE SUMMER DEAL

Twist of Fate

A Heartbreaker Bay Novella

By Jill Shalvis

1001 Dark Nights

EVIL EYE
CONCEPTS

Twist of Fate
A Heartbreaker Bay Novella
By Jill Shalvis

1001 Dark Nights

Copyright 2019 Jill Shalvis
ISBN: 978-1-970077-30-8

Foreword: Copyright 2014 M. J. Rose

Published by Evil Eye Concepts, Incorporated

Sign up for the 1001 Dark Nights Newsletter
and be entered to win a Tiffany Key necklace.

There's a contest every month!

Go to www.1001DarkNights.com to register.

**As a bonus, all subscribers can download
FIVE FREE exclusive books!**

One Thousand and One Dark Nights

Once upon a time, in the future…

*I was a student fascinated with stories and learning.
I studied philosophy, poetry, history, the occult, and
the art and science of love and magic. I had a vast
library at my father's home and collected thousands
of volumes of fantastic tales.*

*I learned all about ancient races and bygone
times. About myths and legends and dreams of all
people through the millennium. And the more I read
the stronger my imagination grew until I discovered
that I was able to travel into the stories… to actually
become part of them.*

*I wish I could say that I listened to my teacher
and respected my gift, as I ought to have. If I had, I
would not be telling you this tale now.
But I was foolhardy and confused, showing off
with bravery.*

*One afternoon, curious about the myth of the
Arabian Nights, I traveled back to ancient Persia to
see for myself if it was true that every day Shahryar
(Persian: شهریار, "king") married a new virgin, and then
sent yesterday's wife to be beheaded. It was written
and I had read, that by the time he met Scheherazade,
the vizier's daughter, he'd killed one thousand
women.*

Something went wrong with my efforts. I arrived in the midst of the story and somehow exchanged places with Scheherazade — a phenomena that had never occurred before and that still to this day, I cannot explain.

Now I am trapped in that ancient past. I have taken on Scheherazade's life and the only way I can protect myself and stay alive is to do what she did to protect herself and stay alive.

Every night the King calls for me and listens as I spin tales. And when the evening ends and dawn breaks, I stop at a point that leaves him breathless and yearning for more. And so the King spares my life for one more day, so that he might hear the rest of my dark tale.

As soon as I finish a story... I begin a new one... like the one that you, dear reader, have before you now.

Chapter 1

Wearing nothing but a pair of jeans and a bad 'tude, Diego Stone lay on the sky bridge of his boat and stared up at the San Francisco sky. It was butt-ass cold, turbulent and moody, all of which suited him just fine.

He had no idea why he'd left sunny, warm, sexy San Diego.

Oh, wait, he did.

He'd received a text asking him to show up for his brother's important, all-hands-on-deck wedding planning lunch that, as Rocco's best man, Diego was required to attend. A text. And not from Rocco, but from his fiancé, Tyler.

Hands behind his head, feet crossed, Diego purposely relaxed his body one inch at a time. It was a technique he'd learned early on during a childhood as tempestuous and unstable as the sky above him. A childhood he'd spent right here in San Francisco.

When he cleared his head the best he could, he rose to get things over with. Being back in town for the next week was going to suck hard, but he knew of only one way to get through shit, and that was to plow straight ahead.

As far as command performances went, he could've tried a little harder to muster up some enthusiasm, but after ten years of being an island of one, he was out of practice at the whole family thing.

The French House at one p.m., the text had said. And, apparently, his presence was both needed *and* required. Funny, because once upon a time when Diego had desperately needed and required Rocco's presence, he hadn't gotten it.

Damn. And here he'd told himself that he was over the past.

He glanced down. He'd spent the past few years running a small boat charter service for a guy who didn't like to get his hands wet. Since Diego loved being on the water, the job had been tailor-made for him. He moonlighted as a tattoo artist as well to keep his skills honed, and he loved that gig, too. But in his current lifestyle, *dressing up* meant tucking a t-shirt into his board shorts.

The French House was a high-end restaurant that he was pretty sure no one in his family had ever been to, but he was willing to bet the place frowned on jeans. Shit. Moving below deck, he stripped and stalked to his closet where he upgraded to black pants and a slate-colored button-down, both of which at least matched his mood. At the last minute, he added a jacket because why get this far, only to get refused at the door.

He borrowed a motorcycle from an old friend and hit the road, still brooding. It'd been a long time since he and Rocco had been in the same room at the same time.

Even longer since they'd been in the same room at the same time without yelling at each other.

When Diego walked into the restaurant, a maître d' with blue, spiked hair and a bowtie greeted him. "I'm here for the Stone wedding planning lunch," he said.

The bowtied maître d', who looked to be around twelve, shook his head. "I don't see a wedding planning lunch... Oh, but I do see a Stone reservation. This way, sir." And then he turned and started walking through the restaurant. The place had been built over the pier in such a way that, combined with all the glass walls, it felt like they were walking right on the waves.

For a guy who lived on the water, it was annoying as shit to feel off balance. Oh, wait, that wasn't the water at all, but the fact that he could see a table nestled in a corner of glass walls just up ahead. A table for four. And three of the seats were occupied. Rocco, his fiancé Tyler, and…a blast from Diego's past that he had thought to never see again.

Daisy Evans.

He staggered back a step as if he'd been shot. Pierced in the damn heart. He put a hand to his chest, shocked to find that he wasn't actually bleeding. Could've fooled him by the amount of pain he was suddenly in.

The three at the table looked cozy. His brother, the guy's fiancé, and the woman Diego had once loved more than life itself leaning into each other, speaking quietly but earnestly, smiling easily, laughing…

Diego realized that he'd stopped in his tracks right in the middle of the restaurant. Rocco glanced over and saw him. "Diego," his brother said, coming to his feet, gesturing him closer.

Diego's feet took him there, though he couldn't seem to tear his gaze from Daisy. Ten years. It was almost too much to process. It'd been ten years, and just the sight of her still rocked him off his axis. With immense difficulty, he tore his gaze off her and looked at his brother.

Rocco grinned. "It's good to see you."

Diego didn't smile or speak. Wasn't even sure he could.

The twelve-year-old-looking maître d' was trying to get him to sit. He'd pulled out the empty chair and was gesturing to it with a flourish of his hand.

Rocco looked at Diego with a half-smile and some worry in his eyes.

He should be a helluva lot more than worried.

Tyler, who Diego had never met, came out of his chair and moved around the table. And then he wrapped Diego up in a hug. The guy was a foot shorter than Diego, but that didn't deter him one bit. He just gave Diego a warm squeeze as if they were old friends and then pulled back—leaving his hands on Diego's arms—as he smiled up into his face. "You're as gorg as the pics promised," he said. "Nice to finally meet you. Won't you sit? We've ordered, I hope you don't mind. But Daisy's on a lunch break from her office and has limited time today."

And then, somehow—Diego would never know how—Tyler gently nudged him into his chair, fussing over him a moment and making sure he had his water and napkin.

Tyler then turned and did the same to Rocco, letting his hands linger. "Darling, you too. Let's sit. Let's toast. Let's lunch. Let's have our little chitchat to clear the air, it'll all be good."

Diego's brother took a deep breath and nodded. Downed a glass of something that was most definitely not champagne. He started to speak but stopped, then swore beneath his breath and rubbed his eyes.

"He's all verklempt," Tyler explained to Diego.

Diego nodded. Same. "So…this wasn't a wedding planning lunch," he said, wishing he had more than a glass of water in front of him. "It's what? An intervention?"

Daisy met Diego's gaze for the first time. Her eyes were still slay-me gray, framed by inky black lashes that drew a man in like she was the only warm haven in a world gone mad. "Diego," she said softly.

"Daisy." Hey, look at that. His voice sounded perfectly calm. Casual. Not at all like his heart was about to pound right out of his chest. The heart she'd once slayed.

"Diego." She didn't seem surprised to see him. As for what her thoughts might be, she kept them damn well hidden, though her voice when she spoke trembled a bit. "Thanks for coming," she said, like this was a normal thing and not the first time they'd seen each other in ten years. "We're all just hoping you and Rocco can talk out any…issues so we can make sure things are smooth for the wedding."

Her voice was still quiet but husky, just as it used to be, the same tone that had given him more sexual fantasies than any other.

But these days, he no longer thought about her. At least, not that he'd admit. "And you're here…why?"

"Because I asked her," Rocco said.

At his older brother's words, Diego cocked his head but didn't take his eyes off Daisy. "Because…?"

"She's our wedding planner," Tyler said smoothly, waving down a waiter and signaling for more wine. "The best in the business."

Daisy smiled at Tyler and then turned back to Diego. "It's nice to see you."

What the hell? He'd fallen asleep on the boat and was dreaming this, right? *Nice to see him?* Was she kidding? He'd told her that he loved her, and then she'd left. Moved to New York for college without looking back. He opened his mouth to remind her of that fact, but Rocco stood up and tugged on his arm.

"I think we should talk outside."

Diego wrenched free without looking at him and turned to Daisy. "I need to talk to you." He had no idea what game she was playing, but he intended to find out.

Daisy opened her mouth to say something, but before she could, Rocco once again put a hand on him.

Diego looked down at his arm. Rocco was older by two years, but at six foot four, Diego had four inches on his brother—most of them harder and leaner. Rocco with his bulkier mass outweighed Diego and was more badass when it came right down to it, but Diego was working on a lot of resentment and anger, so it'd be a solid match.

And a fight long overdue.

Rocco dropped his hand from Diego and shoved his fingers through his shaggy, black hair that was the same as Diego's. Apparently, Rocco had learned some restraint over the years, but not too much as he jerked his head to the door and lumbered out.

Diego followed without looking back.

Which wasn't easy because Daisy had looked…different. Among other things. She'd always been girl-next-door pretty. And part of what Diego had loved about her was that they'd had a lot in common. Both had grown up on the wrong side of the tracks, the poor kids who didn't have a penny to their name.

She was still girl-next-door pretty, but there was a whole new air about her now, as well. She was dressed in a blue suit dress and matching heels, looking professional, smart, and incredibly sure of herself—which he had to admit, was attractive as hell.

But she also looked like someone he didn't know. Certainly not the type of woman who'd mesh with a guy who lived on a boat.

"Well," he heard her say to Tyler as he walked away. "That went about as well as expected."

In response, Tyler laughed softly, apparently unconcerned that his fiancé was about to get the pretty punched off his face.

Ahead of him, Rocco pushed out the restaurant doors and walked down the pier to a relatively isolated spot. Instead of turning to face Diego, his brother leaned on the piling and let out a whoosh of air.

Diego stood behind him, waiting.

Finally, Rocco straightened and faced him.

"Nice blind side," Diego said.

Rocco winced. "I knew you'd take it like that, but Tyler thought a neutral spot would be best."

"Since when is a place like The French House neutral?"

"We both know you wouldn't have come to Dad's house or the tat shop, so I don't know what the hell your problem is."

"My problem," Diego said trying to temper himself, "is that you didn't even try to contact me yourself. And then to sit there like we're having tea with the queen, only it's Daisy, my—" He broke off. *First love?* Hell, first everything. But he wasn't about to say that. "You could have called me."

"You wouldn't have come if I asked." Rocco shook his head. "I should've told you to stay the hell away. Because telling you not to do something makes you do the opposite. You were like that as a kid, too. When Dad told you not to sneak out, you'd do it twice and take pictures."

True. And besides the point. "I agreed to be your best man,"

Diego said. "Why wouldn't I have come?"

"Because we haven't gotten along since the day you took off ten years ago."

"I took off?" Diego repeated in disbelief. "Are you serious? You're rewriting history to suit yourself now."

Rocco took a step toward him and poked a finger in Diego's pec. "You don't know what it was like here alone after Dad died. You're my brother, you should've—"

Diego stepped into Rocco's finger so that they were toe-to-toe, effectively cutting off Rocco's words. "I'm the one who took care of him night and day for two years after his stroke. When he couldn't talk, couldn't move, couldn't care for himself. I was eighteen and in my first semester at college—which I had to junk. Where were you then, *brother*?"

Rocco didn't say anything. Diego knew he couldn't say much since it was all true.

Growing up, Diego and their dad had fought. A lot. Diego got it. He'd been a handful and trouble-bound. Rocco had been just as wild, but he had a way of hiding it, and he'd definitely been the favored son. He and their dad had shared a real relationship that Diego had robbed himself of.

He'd always planned to resolve their issues, he'd just never known how. But time had run out because after their dad's stroke, the guy had been completely nonverbal, and they couldn't resolve shit. At the time, Diego had wanted to keep him in hospice because all medical opinions led to one thing—his dad wasn't going to come back from the stroke. The man had been fiercely proud, and Diego knew that being at home in that condition with his sons having to take care of his personal needs would have killed him even faster. He'd never have wanted to be that helpless in front of them.

But Rocco had disagreed. Vehemently. And one night after Diego had left the hospital, Rocco had checked their dad out. It'd taken him half a day to realize his mistake. That in fact, he wasn't capable of the level of care their dad required. But by then, the insurance wouldn't cover the costs of readmittance—not unless their dad ended up back in the ICU.

The next morning, Diego had woken to find Rocco gone. He'd left a note saying that he had to get away.

Leaving Diego alone and in charge.

And Rocco had stayed gone. Turned out he'd been in the Bahamas, falling in love and finding a life thousands of miles away.

Their dad had died two years later. Diego had waited until the funeral, which Rocco had shown up for. He'd handed Rocco a stack of medical bills and the keys to the house and The Canvas Shop—the tattoo parlor that had been their dad's legacy. "My turn," he'd said and left town.

That had been a decade ago.

Now, they stared at each other until Diego shook his head. "You wanted me here, and I came. Let's just do what has to be done."

That's when Diego heard the click, click, clicking of high heels coming towards them, loud and clear. Even before the wearer of those shoes came around the corner, he knew who it'd be.

Daisy, with her carefully pinned-up hair that he happened to know felt like silk between his fingers. She'd slipped on sunglasses so he couldn't see her eyes, but if the grim set of her pretty, lightly glossed lips was anything to go by, she wasn't nearly as impressed with him as he was with her.

"Look," she said, stopping a few feet back from him and Rocco. "If I'd wanted to watch two men go at each other, I could be doing it from my couch in my PJs with any of my fave reality shows."

There she is, Diego thought. The feisty, sassy, sexiest woman he'd ever met.

Rocco started to speak, but Daisy held up a hand. "This is clearly a family affair, so I'm going home. Rocco, I'll see you tomorrow at the cake testing."

"Daisy," Diego said, her name feeling incredibly rusty on his lips.

She hesitated a moment before meeting his gaze, making him wonder if she felt any of what he did. As for what the hell it was that he felt, he couldn't have put it into words even if someone had a gun to his head. "We need to talk too," he said.

That got him the barest hint of a smile, one completely devoid of humor. "That's me," Daisy quipped lightly. "Always second in the lineup. Why am I not surprised?"

What the hell? *He* was the injured party here, but she strode away as quickly as she'd arrived, leaving him staring after her, stunned.

"Listen," Rocco said. "I know we've had our differences, but I'm getting married next week, and you're my only family. I want you by my side, dammit." He jabbed a thumb toward the restaurant, which thanks to the glass walls, meant they could see inside.

Tyler was still at the corner table, alone now, watching them. When he saw them look his way, he gave a small finger wave and an encouraging smile.

"See that?" Rocco muttered. "He thinks we're civilized enough to be trusted alone with each other simply because we're brothers. That's how his mind works. And I love him ridiculously enough to want him to keep believing that this is going to be okay."

Diego stared at his brother. He hadn't taken the time until this very second to really soak in the sight of the man in front of him, the one he hadn't seen since…well, their dad's funeral.

Christ, *that* had been a day.

"Listen," Rocco said quietly, more seriously, his eyes solemn. "I get it. I shouldn't have tricked you into coming here, calling the lunch a best man's thing. But I just…I just wanted to see you, man. I wanted you to be involved this week leading up to the wedding. I wanted… Shit. I wanted it like old times. I was hoping that maybe this could be a chance for us to put our issues aside. Or, hell, maybe we can even figure them out."

At the unexpected mature side to his brother, Diego took a step back and ran a hand over his face. "When did you grow up?"

Rocco gave a rueful smile. "It started the day I screwed up with you. I've had ten years to perfect it."

Diego drew in a deep breath. "Why is Daisy your wedding planner?"

"She's one of my best friends."

This caught Diego by surprise on a day where he'd thought he couldn't get more surprised. "Since when?"

"Since she came back to the city like five years ago."

Diego could feel his chest tightening. Maybe it was an impending heart attack, because what the actual hell? Diego and Daisy had been best friends and far more, but they'd not managed to keep in touch once they split. Though somehow, his brother who was the king of *not* keeping in touch had taken up a relationship with her. It shouldn't have pissed him off, but it did.

"She's the best at what she does," Rocco said. "I need her. But I need you more."

Diego had no choice here. He wasn't a complete asshole. And if he were being honest, he'd missed Rocco—much more than he was ready to admit. "Okay. You've got me. What do you need?"

Rocco appeared to breathe a sigh of relief. "The first thing is tomorrow's cake tasting. We've had a last-minute change of bakery. Daisy arranged this new one."

"I don't know," Diego said. "If you want this to go smoothly, having me and Daisy in the same room probably isn't a great idea."

"I really need you both there, man."

With a shake of his head, Diego looked out at the water and took a beat to breathe. He was being manipulated, he could feel it. And he hated that. "I'll need to talk to Daisy first."

Rocco pulled out his phone and did something, and from within Diego's pocket, his own cell buzzed. He pulled out the device, eyed the text, and then looked up at his brother.

"Daisy's address." Rocco held his gaze.

"She lives in the same building as The Canvas Shop?"

"Yep. Fourth-floor, one-bedroom apartment. Consider the intel a peace treaty. But, uh…" Rocco grimaced. "Maybe lie about how you got it. No sense in her hating both of us, right?"

Chapter 2

Daisy sat in a conference room at work while her boss, the sole proprietor of an event planning company, droned on about a new event at the opera house in a few months. It was important, and Daisy was trying to pay attention.

But it wasn't work that she had on the brain. Not even close. Nope, all she could see was Diego's face from earlier, just before she'd walked away.

He'd gone from boy to man in the past ten years. It didn't help that he still had a way of drawing her in, even by just standing there on the dock, eyes lit with a restrained temper. Even pissed off, he was all kinds of hot. His body was hard and muscular, with an ass that looked amazing both in and out of jeans. He was six feet plus of pure sexiness, with black hair that fell over his forehead and curled around his collar when it got too long—which it always was. He had eyes the color of well-aged whiskey that darkened whenever he felt something deeply, like anger.

Or arousal…

"Are you even listening to me?" her boss asked, sounding unhappy.

But since that was Carol's default mood, it was hard to tell. The woman was in her seventies, but thanks to good, ahem, *genes*—AKA the best plastic surgeon in the city—she looked mid-fifties. She catered mostly to her own generation, which meant that she wasn't getting younger clients.

That's what Daisy had supposedly been hired for. But it turned out that Carol really didn't want younger clients.

Which left Daisy working a whole lot of fiftieth-anniversary parties. She'd tried to bring in Rocco's wedding, but Carol hadn't been comfortable with it, saying that the timing was too tight.

So, Daisy had happily taken it on herself as a side job. Planning a good friend's wedding seemed infinitely more appealing than some huge IT tech company's annual employee party and the opera event her current workload consisted of. "Sorry, yes, I'm listening," she said with an inward grimace. "And I agree wholeheartedly. The opera event will be wonderful, thank you for trusting me with it."

Carol nodded frostily and started to leave but stopped. "I count on you, Daisy. I hired you because you're focused and you work hard."

"And because you know I don't have a personal life, so I'll work all the overtime you need," Daisy said.

Carol let out a rare smile, small as it was. "Yes. So, don't go getting a life on me now."

Even if Daisy wanted to…

Carol shrugged. "Your good work might pay off in ways you never imagined. You never know."

That was true. One never knew. When Daisy was young, the future had been some intangible thing that she couldn't begin to grasp because she'd been too busy worrying about surviving the present.

Some things never changed. Thirty years old and still worrying about her present.

"In any case, I'll need the specs for the new job by the end of the day," Carol said, turning to walk away. "Hope you don't mind working late tonight."

"Actually, I do."

Carol stopped and raised a brow.

Daisy worked at not quailing. "I've been working since five a.m. because we had that UK phone meeting."

Carol didn't look moved. "And?"

"And...it's going on six p.m." Daisy didn't have a set of balls, but she liked to think the equipment she did have was even tougher. She stood up and shut her laptop, tucking it into her bag. "I'll get back on this first thing in the morning."

Suddenly looking thoughtful, Carol nodded. "I wish I'd had your fiery spirit when I was your age. Things might be different."

"What things?"

Carol turned to look out the window. "Sometimes, I think about giving it all up," she said softly. "And retiring to a warm beach somewhere."

Daisy blinked in shock. "What?"

"Yeah... I'm tired of the rat race. There's got to be an easier way to live." Carol turned and looked at Daisy. "I want you to take over for me."

Daisy just stared at her boss. "But you've worked your whole adult life to build this business. You're booked out solid for two years."

"You can handle it. I've got faith." Carol gave a small, rare smile. "Just say you'll think about it."

Stunned, Daisy nodded. "Of course."

When Carol left, Daisy stood. Still feeling dazed, she grabbed her things and headed out. She didn't lose it until the elevator doors had closed. Only then, knees a little weak at her bravado, she leaned back against the wall and took a few deep breaths.

She'd grown up the perpetual scrappy underdog, so she was good at survival. What she'd never been good at was standing up for herself.

She'd been working on that.

When the elevators opened next, Daisy was once again standing and—hopefully—looking cool and professional as she strode across the lobby and out the front doors of the building to the center of the financial district of downtown San Francisco.

The streets were gridlocked traffic, the sidewalks filled with commuters leaving work and heading home. The hustle and bustle had been a thrill when Daisy came back to her hometown after her college years in New York.

She loved both cities, but…there was no place like home.

She bussed her way to her apartment in the Pacific Pier Building of the Cow Hollow District. Not coincidentally, the same building that housed The Canvas Shop, the tattoo parlor that Rocco had taken over from his and Diego's father.

Diego… Seeing him today had thrown her. She'd known he would be there, of course, but nothing could have prepared her for coming face-to-face with him ten years after he'd broken her heart and then stomped on it for good measure.

So why the hell he'd implied that it'd been *her* to destroy them was beyond her. Just thinking about it had her stewing all over again. She rubbed her aching chest, giving her heart a stern talking to. *Stop getting involved, your job is to pump blood, and that's it.*

It would have helped if Diego hadn't looked so good. Say maybe having lost some of that thick, sinfully wavy dark hair of his so her fingers hadn't itched to sink into it. Or even better, if he'd grown love handles.

But neither of those things had happened. What *had* happened was that Diego had grown into all his long, lean, lanky inches and then some. The boy she'd once known and loved was long gone, not a trace of him left except for those whiskey-colored eyes. The man he'd become—tall, strong, and attitude-riddled—was a stranger to her.

He would stay that way.

And maybe if she repeated it enough to herself, she'd actually believe it.

Getting off the bus, she walked through the cobblestoned

courtyard of her building. Usually, she took her time here, enjoying the glorious old architecture, the corbeled brick and exposed iron trusses, the big windows. But the evening was chilly, and her feet hurt.

She passed The Canvas Shop. Just inside the big picture window, she could see Rocco working on a client, as well as Sadie and Mini Moe, two of his best tattoo artists, as they did the same. Sadie's better half, Caleb, was there too, making everyone laugh.

Sadie had become a dear friend, and Daisy often stopped in at this time of night so they could all order in takeout and share.

But tonight, she needed to be alone.

She took the elevator to the fourth floor because her poor toes were screaming at her. It'd been a case of beauty versus comfort with her heels that morning, and she'd stupidly chosen style.

Letting herself into her apartment, she immediately stripped, put on PJs, and...ate everything in her fridge. Then she put on Netflix and grabbed the ice cream from the freezer.

Some days required more self-care than others.

She'd just gotten comfy when a knock came at her door. Damn. Setting aside the carton of rocky road, she got up, leaned into the peephole and stilled. *Oh shit.*

Diego.

She stepped back and had a pep-talk with herself. *Okay, remember...you are not the sweet, innocent little thing you once were. The one who fell head over heels for that crooked smile. You're a grownup, a professional, and you don't need no stinkin' man—*

He knocked again, and she jumped a little. *What is he doing here?* He'd made it clear earlier what she'd already known, that he hadn't missed her, probably hadn't given her a single thought in all these years.

It rankled that she couldn't say the same, though it wasn't from lack of trying. She'd done her best to get over him, but he'd been soul-deep. And that was hard to exhume.

His voice came again, surprisingly low, but she could hear him clearly enough. "Daisy, I know you're in there. I can smell the wheels burning."

Rolling her eyes at both of them, she opened the door to find him standing there, hands resting above him on the doorjamb, filling the space with that big, tough body that had once upon a time made hers sing the hallelujah chorus.

He lifted his head, his eyes meeting hers. "Yeah, trust me, I'm not thrilled either," he said. "What was that crack about me putting you second?"

"Why do you care?"

Looking surprised, he opened his mouth but then shut it again with a small shake of his head as if he couldn't process her question. Instead of answering, he brushed past her to enter.

"Gee," she said dryly. "Come on in."

He looked around the small but cozy apartment she loved because it was home in a way no other place had ever been. She could tell that he didn't miss anything, including the fact that her TV was paused on Netflix, there was a gallon of ice cream sitting open on the coffee table with a wooden spoon sticking out of it, and a slightly embarrassingly large glass of wine sat nearby. He turned to face her.

Yes, she knew what he'd been up to. Her stalking skills were even better than her event planning skills, and she prided herself on being the best at that. He had an Instagram account that he was annoyingly stingy about posting on, but she'd managed to learn some things. Such as when she left for New York to take her scholarship, he'd stayed here in San Francisco, taking care of his dad after his debilitating stroke and running The Canvas Shop. After his dad's death, Diego had left for San Diego, and as far as she could tell, he'd not been back since.

Until now.

"I care," Diego said, startling her.

"Huh." She nodded. "You've got a funny way of showing it."

He stood still, watching her, his energy deceptively relaxed.

Because he wasn't. Relaxed. It'd been nearly a decade since she'd been wrapped around that gorgeous body, but she still knew it almost better than she knew her own.

"I thought we should talk," he said.

"Okay, and here's what I think," she said carefully. "One, you're the best man of your brother's wedding. Two, I'm the wedding planner. Three, we're doing this for Rocco. And none of those things are going to change, correct?"

He nodded curtly.

"So then, we have no choice," she said. "We have to get through this. I suggest we make a pact."

"A pact."

"Yes," she said.

His eyes darkened, and just like that, she was thrown back in time to the way they'd been. Young. Sweet. Ridiculously in love. And competitive as hell. They'd made a lot of pacts in those days. Actually, more like dares. Who could outrun the other to the pier and back. Who could get their homework done the fastest. Who could make better cinnamon and sugar toast... Each bet had come with a prize—winner's choice, of course. And since neither ever had a cent to their name, the bounty had almost always been sexual.

She'd often counted on it.

The memories in his gaze had her swallowing hard. "The pact is we avoid each other whenever possible," she said.

Now, he looked amused. "How do you suggest we do that when we're going to be in the same room more often than not?"

"We both know there are ways to avoid someone even if they're standing right next to you."

This got her another long look from him, and she lifted her chin. "I suggest we start right now."

When he didn't respond to that, she picked up her glass of wine and drank it all. Liquid courage and all that. "I'm going to take your silence as agreement." She set down the now-empty glass. "So, let's call this happy reunion over and done so you can let me get back to my life."

"It's seven o'clock, and you're in your PJs drinking wine and eating ice cream by the gallon. And your Netflix screen is flashing '*do you want to keep watching*' messages."

She narrowed her eyes. "Maybe my social life is so full that this is the first night I've been alone in forever. Maybe I just want to Netflix and chill without talking."

He just looked at her for a long beat, not saying a word, but she could once again see a tiny smile lurking at the corners of his mouth. This time, the expression was devoid of sarcasm and far more genuine. Warm, even. Which led to other thoughts about that sexy mouth of his.

Wait. *Stop*. Dammit. Note to self: *no more wine while Diego's in town!*

Instead of leaving, he took the few steps to close the space between them, making her suck in a breath because there'd always been something about being this close to him, something that constantly had her body humming just beneath her skin with anticipation and hunger and need.

She'd told herself it was because he'd been her first love, and a girl never forgot *that* guy. But why in the world did she still feel it? Managing to not take a step back—or let's be honest, a step into him—she kept herself still except to tilt her head back to meet his gaze. "What?"

"We'll play this your way," he said quietly. "We'll do our best to avoid each other."

"Good."

He nodded once. "But—"

"No buts," she said quickly.

"But..." he went on, undeterred, "if you ever want to Netflix and chill without talking with a warm body next to yours, let me know."

She was still staring at him in utter shock when he gave a quick shake of his head like he was amused and also annoyed by both of them, before walking out and quietly closing the door behind him.

Chapter 3

Diego might have lived in San Diego for the past few years, but he still had friends in San Francisco. He'd grown up here, in more ways than one, and sometimes it was the early connections one made that stuck more than others.

Wes had been Diego's childhood best friend. He now ran a mechanic shop in the Castro district, and it was he who'd lent Diego the Harley. After coercing Diego into buying him a late dinner, Diego had taken the Harley on a long drive throughout the city. Because, for some reason, he'd thought that going down Memory Lane would be a good idea.

Newsflash, it wasn't.

He went to North Beach and idled on a quiet street in front of a small Victorian home. He and Rocco had grown up in that house. Their mom had died when Diego was a baby, and he didn't remember anything about her, which he'd long ago convinced himself was for the best. His earliest memory was of being five years old and climbing the tree in the front yard after his dad had told him not to. Not ten minutes later, he'd fallen out of the tree and broken his arm.

But even remembering the sickening pain of having the bones

reset hadn't taught him to listen to his dad.

He'd been twelve when he snuck out with some pilfered booze and ended up in the garage with the fifteen-year-old, much wiser twin girls from next door. His dad had beaten the shit out of him for that one, but even that couldn't take away the smile and experience that garage visit had given him.

By fifteen, Diego had pretty much run wild and free. He'd landed in trouble at school with grades and other things, and he'd been given a choice—be expelled, or straighten up and turn his shit around. Fast.

So, he'd tried to turn his shit around.

His dad had arranged for tutoring, and his life had been forever changed by the sweetest, kindest girl he'd ever met.

Daisy.

As it happened, she'd had it just as rough growing up as he had, only she wasn't constantly toeing the line—or worse, trying to obliterate it. She just quietly and unassumingly took in everything she could to make sure that she had the tools she needed to make it out.

And she'd done just that, leaving him behind. And with some dubious maturity, he couldn't even be mad. He was proud of her. Proud as hell.

But, damn. He still missed her.

* * * *

The next morning, Diego parked Wes's bike in the bakery lot. Bracing himself for another battle, he strode inside for the dreaded cake tasting. He was right on time, which was why he was surprised to find the place empty.

The door opened behind him, and he knew without even turning around who the clicking heels belonged to.

Daisy came up to his side and eyed the empty place. "Huh," she said and pulled out her phone to check the time. "Huh," she said again.

"Maybe Rocco and Tyler eloped," he said hopefully.

She snorted and muttered something beneath her breath that sounded suspiciously like, "I couldn't possibly have gotten that lucky."

"Hey," he said, turning to her. "I'm a delight."

She managed to keep a straight face for a full second before she laughed.

And while he wanted to be annoyed as hell, he couldn't. Because...her laugh. It was like fresh grass after the rain. A wide-open road late at night with a full tank of gas and a full moon. It was both Heaven and Hell. Because, damn. He didn't want to be moved by her laugh. He didn't want to be moved by her at all.

A young woman came out from the back of the shop and smiled at them from behind the front counter. "How can I help you?"

"We're here for a cake tasting appointment," Daisy said. "For Rocco Stone and Tyler Houston."

The woman nodded and opened a laptop to check her schedule. "Yes, I've got everything set up for the two of you." She smiled at them. "You're going to make a gorgeous wedding couple."

"Oh, no, we're not the couple," Daisy said quickly with a laugh as if it was the most ridiculous, asinine thing that they might be a couple. Even though, once upon a time, she'd promised Diego forever.

She'd either forgotten, or she was enjoying twisting the knife.

"I'm the wedding planner," Daisy went on, then made a vague gesture at Diego. "And he's the best man." Her phone buzzed from inside her purse. "Excuse me a minute," she said, fishing out her cell. She looked at the screen and then at Diego before answering. "Rocco. You and Tyler running late?" She paused, head tilted as she listened, her eyes slowly narrowed. "Uh-huh... Traffic on Divisadero...okay, sure, hold on." She held out her phone to Diego. "He wants to talk to you."

Diego put the cell to his ear and let his silence speak for him.

"Listen," Rocco said quietly as if trying to keep Tyler from overhearing him. "So, we're stuck in traffic. We're not going to make it."

Diego responded to the bullshit story with more silence.

"So…here's the thing," Rocco went on when he clearly got that Diego wasn't going to make it easy. "Daisy is one of my dearest friends. I love her madly, but she's going to side with Tyler on everything. I need your opinion in there. So, can you hang out and make sure I don't get some sort of mango filling with a green tea cake or something like that? Oh, and no flowers on the cake, okay? Nothing frou-frou. And we don't need any fancy, high-tiered cake with a figurine on the top either. None of that gay shit. And, yeah, I know, I heard it as I spoke, but I like what I like."

"You really think you should trust me with all that?" Diego asked, feeling a twinge of amusement.

"Please," Rocco said, sounding sincerely worried. "Nothing frou-frou."

Diego took great satisfaction out of disconnecting without making any promises. He looked up at the baker. "All right, let's get this over with."

Daisy slid him a dirty look, which he returned with an innocent *what* look of his own.

"Be nice," she mouthed.

The baker smiled nervously and turned to lead them to a table decked out with champagne and testing-size cakes galore. "We've got all sorts of different things to try," she said. "But is there anything you'd like to start with?"

"Let's just go with the basics," Diego said. "No reason to make this a whole big drawn-out thing and keep you from…baking."

"Oh, no worries," she said with a smile. "We set aside an hour and a half for each couple's cake tasting."

Diego blinked in disbelief. *An hour and a half?* "Are you serious?"

Daisy shot him another look. "This is serious, you can't just blow through this like you do everything else." She turned to the baker. "Tyler, one of the grooms, was hoping for mango filling. And he was very interested in green tea-flavored cake. He said you had cupcakes like that, and they were the most delicious things he'd ever tasted."

The baker nodded enthusiastically and looked over at Diego. "And the other groom…?"

Diego smiled, suddenly feeling a whole lot better about the day. "He'd want to make Tyler happy."

Daisy took in his smile and blinked before biting her lower lip.

The way she used to when she wanted to be kissed.

And, just like that, he went from smug as hell to…damn. Something else entirely.

The baker took in the strained silence between them and jumped up. "Let me get us some samples!"

When she was gone, Daisy leaned across the table. "You're up to something."

Most definitely, babe. Not that he could remember *what* at the moment. She was probably completely unaware that her blouse gaped, revealing swells of creamy breasts and a strip of cream-colored lace that matched her skin and made his mouth water.

"Diego," she whispered warningly, her eyes suspicious.

He just smiled, and then the baker was back with samples of green tea cake with mango filling. They both dove in, taking their first bite at the same time. Diego nearly choked on his, having to fight to not visibly recoil.

But not Daisy. She moaned in pleasure and then licked her fork. And then her lips… "This is the one," she said.

"I'll make a note," the baker said with a nod. "But you still have a lot of time left and a bunch of other options to try."

"Great!" Daisy said happily, and Diego couldn't help but smile at her.

Back when they'd been together, they'd eaten cheaply. Ramen. Apples and peanut butter. Whatever they had to do. She'd loved saving a penny, loved free shit. Apparently, she still did.

It was way too fucking cute.

But that wore off quickly. A painfully long hour—and way too much sugar—later, the baker was *finally* writing up the order for green tea cake with mango filling. "How many tiers?"

"Oh," Daisy said, lighting up. "Tyler loves tiers. Maybe three?"

They both looked at Diego, who was still fighting his physical responses to Daisy enjoying her cake.

"No tiers," Rocco had said.

"Three sounds good," Diego said. "Maybe even four. So, we're done here, right?"

Daisy gave him another look.

The baker seemed startled. "Well, not exactly. There's cake toppers. We've got everything from collectible figures to—"

"Figurines," Daisy said, sneaking another bite of cake, once again licking her lips and the fork. "Tyler loves to collect. Two men, of course."

They both looked at Diego.

Since he was having a hard time thinking past the sweet glide of Daisy's tongue along the fork, he simply nodded.

"Done," the baker said, smiling widely, typing on her tablet as fast as she could. "This is wonderful. Everyone happy?"

"Very," Daisy said.

They both looked over at Diego, who needed a sharp stick to stab himself with.

"What do you think?" the baker asked.

What did he think? He thought that his testosterone levels had dropped dangerously just sitting there. Standing, he fished out a credit card, which he thrust at the baker. "Let's get this done."

Five minutes later, Daisy was glowering at him as they exited the bakery. "You couldn't have been any more obnoxious."

"You underestimate me."

She snorted. "Seriously, you're such an a—"

"Amazing brother?"

"I was going to say asshole."

They were in front of the bike now. Daisy had parked next to him.

"Just...take in the big picture here," she said.

"Which is what? That Rocco and Tyler ditched us here today on purpose for who knows what reason other than to torture me?"

She rolled her eyes. "I like how you assume you're the only one being tortured."

"Hey, I've been nothing but a—"

"I swear to God if you say delight..."

He shrugged.

She sighed, looking a little overheated and frustrated and ticked off, which made two of them.

Except he was also turned on. He couldn't help it. Daisy talked with her hands, her eyes flashing. She looked sexy as hell.

"Look," she said. "Rocco's in love. He's marrying the man of his dreams, so it's not about you or me. Or us. Or the utter lack of an us—"

"Funny, because it feels a whole bunch like it's about us," he said.

She opened her mouth to argue that—because God forbid she not argue with every little thing he said—and he decided he'd had enough. So, he pulled her to him and put his mouth over hers.

He'd meant to shut her up, of course, but what he hadn't intended was to forget himself, the wedding, his brother, and everything but the soft little sound that escaped her throat just before she fisted her hands in his shirt.

Going to shove me away or pull me in, babe?

She kissed him back. More than that, she pressed all those sweet, sexy curves up against him. With a groan, he wrapped his arms around her, feeling every contour of her sweet bod against his. Her mouth had started out icy cold from the chill in the air, but it was hot now. They were both hot.

She made another little sound, a sweet little mewl of pleasure that shot straight through him. That alone tamed his inner caveman, and an unexpected tenderness and sense of affection hit him hard.

He cupped her face, his thumbs lightly brushing against her cheeks to kiss her again with a soul-searing gentleness he hadn't even known he possessed.

"Diego," she whispered, and he blinked, shocked to find that he had her pressed up against her car. She had her hands beneath his shirt now, one of them resting over his heart, the other low, nearly at the waistband of his jeans. Even as he thought it, her fingers lightly danced over his abs, which quivered at her touch.

For a beat, they just stared at each other, both breathing heavily, neither moving. Except for her fingers, which seemed extremely eager to go south. With a groan, Diego caught her hand in his. "Playing with fire."

She yanked her palm free and lightly banged the back of her head against her driver's side window a few times.

"What are you doing?"

"Trying to knock something loose," she said. "Like my good sense." Lifting her head again, she gave him a light push on the chest.

She wanted space.

Fine by him. He stepped back but didn't go far.

"You're looking at me like I'm a ticking time bomb," she said.

"You are."

"Flattering."

"Look…" He tried to access any part of his working brain, but there appeared to have been a shutdown across the board, all circuits down. "That—"

"Can't happen again," she said and nodded. "Agreed." She paused. "That's what you were about to say, right?"

Actually, no.

"Because it can't," she said slowly, looking a little uncertain as she took in his expression.

"When did you come to that conclusion?" he asked. "When you had your tongue shoved down my throat, or when you yanked my shirt up to get to bare skin?"

Her mouth went tight. "When you stopped kissing me and

started talking." She pointed at him. "We made a pact to stay as clear of each other as possible through this. Let's stick to it." And then she got in her car and drove away.

The theme song of his life.

Chapter 4

The next day, Daisy got up early because eating ice cream for dinner as she had been lately required hitting the gym a few days a week. She was on the treadmill for an hour and a half before she looked down to check the screen. She'd only been on it for four minutes.

It was going to be one of those days.

When she got to the office, she worked her fingers to the bone with Carol on her back about more incoming bids, more clients, more, more, more…making Daisy question whether she would ever really retire.

"Of course, she's not going to retire," Daisy's best friend from college said, video chatting Daisy during a quick lunch break from New York City where Poppy worked at a large corporate concierge firm. "She's just dangling a carrot to keep you from entertaining other offers."

"I have no other offers," Daisy said with a laugh, shoving the last of her sandwich into her mouth.

"Well…" Poppy gave her a hopeful smile. "I've already planned out my New Year's resolution. It's a doozy. You ready to hear it?"

Daisy's New Year's resolution was to put the clothes she tried on every morning back on hangers and into her closet instead of on the chair in the corner of her room. "Sure."

"Well...I've been thinking. You're unhappy there. I'm unhappy here. And we both do basically the same thing. So, why not—?"

"Run away to an island beach somewhere and become barmaids?"

"Or...you come here, and we start our own business. And before you say no," Poppy said quickly, opening her second laptop and swiveling the screen to face Daisy, "I've been putting together some numbers and specs. I think we could rock our own event planning company here in NYC. You're always saying how much you miss the city—and me."

Daisy had absolutely loved New York. A lot. Going across the country at eighteen had freed her from a rough family life and upbringing. It'd given her an education. A different view of the world than her previous narrowed one. But...she loved being back in San Francisco, too. "Poppy..."

"Wait," Poppy said quickly, holding up a hand. "Don't say no off the cuff. Just promise you'll think about it?"

"I will if you promise to think about doing exactly as you've just said but here in San Francisco."

Poppy bit her lower lip, clearly thinking and thinking hard. "Okay, here's what we're going to do. You make me a proposal for San Fran, and I'll finish making mine for NYC. But, FYI, mine's going to be irresistible."

Daisy laughed, but it faded quickly when she heard her boss coming. "Gotta go," she whispered and disconnected just in time.

Carol swept into the room. "Did you get the two new client portfolios I sent over? What do you think? Have you contacted them yet? And start a prelim report."

Daisy checked her email. They'd literally just come in three minutes ago. "Uh—"

Carol's brows rose. "Do I need to put Melinda on the job?"

Melinda was Daisy's nemesis. "Nope, I've got it."

"Great," Carol said and strode out.

Daisy leaned forward and thunked her head on the desk. After a moment, she went back to work and didn't surface for hours, not until her personal cell phone buzzed. She looked over at it and grimaced.

DO NOT ANSWER was calling…

Yesterday after the cake tasting fiasco, which was how she referred to that holy cow kiss they'd shared after the actual cake testing, she'd changed Diego's name in her contacts to *DO NOT ANSWER.*

Just to remind herself.

Plus, it'd been her way of taking control of her tumbling reactions to him. And there were many: regrets, resentment, desire, hunger… It was shocking how just one touch of his incredible mouth had set her emotional maturity back an entire decade.

And he was calling her. Why? She thought of how he'd melted her with his mouth and blew out a breath. She'd never been able to ignore him. So, she answered. "Yes?"

There was a brief pause before he said, "Do you always answer your phone in that irritated-as-all-hell voice, or is that just for me?"

If her voice was irritated as all hell, *his* was not. It was low, husky, and achingly familiar, and it caused all sorts of reactions inside her body—including weak knees, which really pissed her off.

She *was* over him.

She was *over* him.

She was over *him.*

And maybe if she kept repeating that to herself, she'd learn to actually believe it. "What do you want?"

"The groom just informed me that I'm supposed to go by the tuxedo place for a seven p.m. appointment and get fitted. And that I'm not allowed to go alone."

Daisy laughed. Hard to believe after the day she'd had and the messy tangle of emotions he caused within her, but she laughed so hard she snorted.

"Please, have fun with this at my expense," he said dryly.

"Oh, I am." She managed to get a hold of herself. "Rocco's probably worried you'll skip the fitting and attend the wedding in jeans and motorcycle boots. Why can't he go with you?"

"He's got a tattoo client."

"Hmm," she said. "And Tyler?"

"With an interior decorating client."

As she had yesterday, she got an odd feeling. It just wasn't like either of the grooms to miss appointments like this. Both of them were invested and would want to be there to see Diego's suit for the wedding.

"So? Are you coming with me or not?"

"I wasn't aware you'd actually asked me to come," she said, wanting to hear him do just that.

"Will you pretty please come?" he asked, voice low and husky and…dammit.

Note to self: not quite ready for primetime bantering with Diego. "The pact…"

"This is part of our promise to Rocco, Princess," he said. The use of her old nickname had her smile fading, replaced by memories that softened her into a boneless heap of hormones.

"I'm busy," she said. "I'm at work."

"Take a dinner break. Hell, I'll even feed you."

"I'm in the middle of something."

"I'm sure your boss will understand. Everyone's entitled to a break, especially on a long day like you've put in."

"My boss understands no such thing," she said. "And how do you know I'm putting in a long day?"

"Is there another reason you're grumpy?"

Yes. Memories of Diego had kept Daisy up all night. Memories of him moving over her in bed, his eyes locked with hers, both of them lost in each other… "Never mind," she said. "I'll meet you there."

"I'm outside waiting for you."

She gaped at her phone. "How did you know you'd convince me

to go with you?"

"Because you love Rocco and Tyler, remember? And you're bossy and controlling. You want to make sure I get into a damn tux."

Dammit. Because, one…true. And two, just the thought of him in a tux had her head swimming. "I'll be right down."

Five minutes later, she was standing on the sidewalk gawking at him on the Harley, looking…well, edible to be honest.

"Get on," he said and held out a helmet.

She quivered with excitement that she didn't want to admit. The last time she'd been on a bike had been with him. Hell, the *only* time she'd been on a motorcycle had been with Diego. And sometimes, even now, she dreamed about it. About the power of the machine beneath her, the strength of the man she'd wrapped herself around to be her anchor. The wind in her face. Her inner thighs snuggled up to the outside of his. The heightened sense of thrill and awareness and desire and hunger pounding through her as they took the open road…

Diego waited with a patience that was new. He'd changed. Grown up. But he'd also known that being on the back of a bike with him would turn her on. She had no idea if he remembered any of their past with the same longing that she did. She looked into his face, trying to read him, but he wasn't giving anything away. His body was still, all that carefully harnessed and leashed power and control at rest. But then she lifted her gaze to his and sucked in a breath. There was a fire there. And smoke.

And a whole bunch of trouble if she wanted it.

Clearing her throat, she looked down at herself. Thankfully, she was in trousers, but her heels might be a problem. Her blouse was thin, and so was her fitted blazer. Even as she thought it, he shrugged out of his leather jacket and wrapped it around her. Then he took the helmet from her fingers and put it on her head himself, leaning in close with a look of concentration as he attached and adjusted the strap.

While she was still speechless, he did what she hadn't, he zipped up the jacket, right to her chin, then left his hands on her to straighten the collar. Even when that was done, his warm fingers slid up her neck as their gazes locked.

When her breath caught audibly, his thumbs lightly stroked where her pulse raced at the hollow of her throat.

She wanted another kiss. With a shocking amount of yearning, she wanted that. But Diego dropped his hands and gave a nod of his chin for her to get on.

So, that's what she did.

"Hold on," he said, and she slid her arms around his waist and set her chin on his shoulder. As he roared off into the night, she found herself smiling for the first time all day.

He turned his head slightly. "Okay?"

She tightened her grip. "Very."

* * * *

Thirty minutes later, she watched Diego walk out of the dressing room, a dark scowl on his gorgeously scruffy face, his hair a little bit tousled, giving him an overall wild look that went with the tux shockingly well. He could've graced the cover of any bridal magazine, and women the world over would have drooled all over him.

Daisy liked to think that she was above such things, but she closed her mouth just in case.

"No," he said. "Just, no."

"What's no?"

He gestured a hand down his smoking bod. "All of it. It's not happening. Skinny-leg pants? What, am I a twelve-year-old? And the shirt's way too tight, I can't move in it." He turned to the tailor waiting at nervous attention a few feet away. "What else have you got?"

The guy glanced over at Daisy, the whites of his eyes showing, his silent plea for help practically a scream.

Diego just strode over to the racks. "I'll find something myself."

Daisy held up a finger to the terrified tailor and pulled out her cell. She called Rocco. Normally, she'd talk the groomsman down and put some good sense into him, but in this case, Diego was right.

Although the man could look good in—or out—of anything, she saw his point. The suit didn't…well, suit him. It was cut for a much smaller, much more slender man. Don't get her wrong, the way the cut of the pants hugged his world-class ass was something to behold. The shirt, stretched to almost beyond its limits by his shoulders, made her want to lick him from chin to belt buckle and beyond. But…he was clearly uncomfortable, and she had no idea how he was even breathing in that shirt without busting it open at the seams. Since he was the only groomsman, she didn't see what it would hurt to get him into something that he'd be more comfortable in.

Rocco picked up on the first ring. "Let me guess. He didn't show."

"Nope, he's here. But we're going to have to go in a different direction for his suit."

Rocco paused for a weirdly awkward amount of time, almost as if he'd put her on mute to have a conversation with someone. Then he was back. "I trust you and your judgement," he finally said.

A *very* unlike Rocco statement.

"Is Tyler there?" Daisy asked.

"Uh…no. Why?"

He was lying. Tyler was there. Which meant that Rocco wasn't stuck at work tattooing a client that he couldn't cancel on.

Which also meant they could have been here if they'd wanted.

So…why weren't they?

"I had a feeling he wouldn't like the suit," Rocco said. "That's why I asked you to go along."

"Or you could have made sure to be here."

"Yeah, but that's why I hired you," Rocco said smoothly. "Plus, you're good at managing him."

She looked across the room and saw Diego standing there in another suit that the tailor had coaxed him into, looking hot as hell.

"You're kidding, right?" she asked softly. "Manage him? Hello, have you met him?" One did not simply *manage* Diego. Not if one valued their life.

Besides, if she'd had *any* ability to handle him in any possible way, she'd never have let him go.

And, wow. That thought had Daisy staggering back a few feet to sink into a chair. It took her a few minutes to remember that she knew how to breathe.

She disconnected with Rocco and pushed aside an odd sense of suspicion that *she* was the one being managed—by the grooms. She moved toward Diego, who was facing the mirror, so she was able to look her fill. "It looks great on you," she said, sounding a little breathier than she'd like.

She lifted her gaze and found his in the mirror.

His brows rose. "You were just staring at my ass."

Since there was amusement in his gaze and tone, and since she'd been caught ogling, there was no sense in playing coy. She shrugged. "So?"

His smile came out to play. "Like what you see?"

He was teasing her, and that easygoing side of him was the one she'd once fallen for. "I think we can all agree," she said to the tailor, "this is the suit."

"I'll make the adjustments," the tailor said with a nod. Removing the measuring tape from around his neck, he stepped close to Diego.

Diego slid him a look that had the poor tailor swallowing hard as he crouched low to measure for the hem.

Daisy shook her head at Diego.

Over the tailor's head, he grinned. *Grinned.* Good Lord. He was in flirt mode, lighting up her world like he used to.

The tailor was still crouched in front of Diego, a few pins in his mouth, eyes narrowed in concentration as he fiddled with the fit of the pants.

All while Daisy's gaze was held prisoner by Diego's.

"You never answered the question," he said, tone casual, eyes not at all relaxed.

Did she like what she saw?

She waited until the tailor moved away so that Diego could get out of the suit.

But he didn't move. He was waiting for an answer.

"You know I do," she said quietly. "Just as I know you like what you see."

His smile was real now. "I definitely do. You grew up real nice, Princess. I especially like the new…"

He paused, and she narrowed her eyes. If he said boobs or butt—which were *all* hers by the way—she was going to have to slug him.

"Confidence." He cocked his head and studied her. "I think that's my favorite part."

And while she was still gaping at him, he turned and walked into the dressing room.

When he came out in his street clothes a few minutes later, he pulled out a credit card for the tailor and looked at Daisy. "I need dinner after that nightmare."

The tailor looked startled at the *nightmare* part but finished ringing them up and then let them go with what appeared to be relief.

Diego looked at Daisy.

"I could eat," she admitted.

They got back onto the bike. Diego handled the evening traffic with ease, and she relaxed against him, letting the long day catch up to her. She was lost in the sensation of his easy strength and warmth and the rumble of the engine when she realized that he'd parked.

In front of Weener Works on the pier.

Weener Works created the best and most original gourmet hotdogs on the planet, and…it'd been their choice of place to eat back when they were together. They had memories here. They'd played pinball here. They'd competed at all the games, in fact, and she'd held her own. They'd made out in the back booth. He'd asked her to be his girlfriend at the front window table…

"Problem?" he asked when she hesitated to get off the bike.

"Nope." She ordered double cheese fries and a loaded hotdog.

He doubled the order and added a large chocolate milkshake, to go. It was crowded, so while they waited to be served, they hit pinball.

She won.

He took it good-naturedly, laughing and giving her an easy, one-armed celebratory hug that hit her like a bolt of lightning. She froze.

So did he.

They stared at each other, and before she could get control of her limbs, both of her arms slid around his broad shoulders. She let herself have the moment of victory, pushing close in a full-body hug. Her face pressed into his throat, his several-day-old scruff scraping deliciously against her skin. He smelled like Heaven.

When she pulled back, he was looking into her face like he wasn't quite sure what to do with her.

He could join her club.

When their food came, they did what they'd always done. They walked down the pier and found a quiet place to eat while looking out over the water.

It was like a security blanket, the bay sprawled out in front of her, eating her favorite takeout, and sitting next to the one person who'd always gotten her. "I haven't been here since…" She tried to remember and then closed her mouth. The last time she'd been at the pier had been with him.

"Me either," he said quietly.

She looked at him. "Do you miss it here?"

Holding her gaze, he shook his head. "I didn't let myself think about it. When I left, I…" He shrugged. "Left. Mentally and physically."

She nodded. She got that. She just wished it hadn't happened like it did.

She took her last bite and pushed away her basket, leaning back in satisfaction before realizing that he was watching her. "What?"

He smiled. "Nothing."

That was a lie, so she looked down at herself. When Diego first picked her up, she'd been work-ready. Now, hours later, she'd shucked her blazer, the top few buttons of her blouse were undone, her hair was down, and...her face felt achy from all the smiling and laughing.

When she looked up again, he was still watching her in that way he did, like he was both happy to be with her and surprised at feeling that way.

"You lost the stick up your ass," he said. "You let yourself relax around me. I like it."

She'd opened her mouth at the stick comment, but his next words disarmed her.

"We're still attracted to each other."

And he was still blunt as always. But Daisy saw no use denying it. "But we both know that physical chemistry, no matter how off the charts, isn't what's important."

"What is important?"

She lifted a shoulder. "Honesty. Communication. Real friendship."

"Are you saying we didn't have that?" he asked.

"I thought we did, but..." She shook her head. "At the end of the day, no, we didn't have that."

"We didn't even stay friends."

She laughed mirthlessly. "I didn't want to be your friend. I wanted to run you over with a car." Needing a distraction, she gathered up their trash. "So, you're not staying at Rocco's."

He let her change the subject with a small shake of his head. "Didn't want to ruin anything for him, not this week."

She cocked her head and studied him. "You grew up."

He shrugged. "By trial and error, maybe. Mostly error. Like a shitload of error." He smiled when she laughed again. "I'm staying on my boat." Standing, he pulled her up and turned her to the railing. Moving in behind her, he pointed at the marina. "See that dock?

Third one on the right?"

"You always wanted to live on a boat," she breathed, incredibly aware of his body behind hers, guarding it against the chilly wind.

"I did." He took his eyes off the water and looked down at her. "So. A wedding planner, huh?"

"An event planner."

"It fits you," he said. "You were always the one putting together all the parties and bonfires."

"And you're working on boats instead of at the family business."

"You know I never wanted to carry on my dad's legacy."

Daisy did know that. But Diego had been pressured. Big time. "I'd love to see your boat."

They got there in ten minutes. He helped her aboard and then moved ahead of her to give her the tour. At the bow, he helped her climb up to the upper deck, where they lay back to stare up at the gorgeous sky.

"It's been a while," she murmured.

He came up on an elbow and looked down at her and not up at the sky. "Yeah," he agreed softly. "Too long of a while."

She slid her gaze to him, and at the look in his eyes, her entire body tingled with awareness and anticipation and desire. "Diego?" she whispered.

"Yeah?"

"There's something else I want you to show me," she murmured and pulled him down over her.

Chapter 5

Diego braced his weight over Daisy, hands on either side of her face, which was turned up to his. The look in her eyes whipped the smoldering heat between them to a raging, zero-percent-contained wildfire.

And maybe...*maybe* he still could've resisted if she hadn't kissed him like he was literally her salvation. Maybe. But probably not. He'd never been able to deny her. "Daisy—"

"Don't say no," she murmured and rocked that sweet body up against his, all those warm curves he'd dreamed about more than he cared to admit. Say no? He didn't have that kind of willpower.

So, he lowered himself to her and let their desire collide, chest to chest, hips to hips, one of his thighs nestled between hers. He had no idea what he thought he was doing. None. All he knew was that he had to have her. Even knowing this was a one-night thing, even knowing how much it would hurt afterwards, he didn't care about anything but this, tonight, and he intended to make it last as long as possible. With that being his last rational thought, he dipped his head.

Her mouth trembled open, but he went for the hollow of her throat instead, kissing the soft skin there, then tracing his tongue over the spot before making his way to the crook of her neck. When she moaned, he scraped his teeth over her, and she gasped out his name as he sucked the patch of flesh into his mouth, fighting a burning desire to mark her as his.

But she wasn't.

So, instead, he gently kissed that same spot again, slipping a hand under her shirt, running his palm up her stomach to just below her breasts. With another whimper of wanting, she arched into his hand—a silent demand if he'd ever heard one. So, he obeyed and cupped her breast, his thumb gliding over the already hardened peak.

She looked at him with those see-all gray eyes, and he couldn't think beyond the fact that he needed to kiss her, which he did, deeply. She had her hands beneath his shirt now too, one over his heart, which was threatening to pound right out of his chest. Could she feel how out of control he was?

But then she got into his jeans and wrapped her fingers around him, and if he'd thought he was in trouble before... "Daisy." His voice was practically a growl. "Babe. I don't think—"

She stroked.

He groaned and dropped his forehead to hers. "You sure?"

She stroked him again.

Okay, she was sure.

She was trying to shove his jeans down and get his shirt off all at the same time when he again caught her hands and waited until her gaze met his.

"I'm sure!" She sounded slightly crazy and maybe a little exasperated, and he smiled.

"*Now*," she demanded, arching into him. "Here."

"Now," he agreed and rose to his feet. "But not here."

He took her below deck. They landed on his bed in a tangle of sheets. The only light came from the moonlight slanting in through the high, narrow windows, but it was enough to see.

She looked as beautiful in his bed as he remembered. He wanted to go slow and easy, but his good intentions vanished once he stripped and crawled up the bed to assist her in doing the same. One kiss plus the glide of her arms and legs around him as if she were trying to claim him as her own, and he was lost. Lost in her. Lost in them.

Just like always.

He'd always thought if he ever got lucky enough to be with her again, that it might be awkward, like a first time. But it didn't feel awkward or like a first time. It felt more like finding a missing piece.

Like coming home.

He slipped a hand between her thighs. Good thing they were already lying down, or he'd have probably dropped to his knees. In his dreams, he'd had to work hard to make her want him again.

But she was hot and slick and ready.

Her eyes were big but bold on his. "I want you," she whispered. "I've…always wanted you."

It wasn't a declaration of love, so why did it feel like one? Because his own feelings were far too close to the surface, dangerously close in fact. "I've always wanted you too, Daisy."

They reached for each other at the same time, the kiss intense and lingering. "Now," she murmured. "*Please*, Diego."

Like he could deny that breathy plea. Shifting, he kissed and nibbled and licked, and then nibbled some more as he made his way down her body, absorbing her soft sighs, smiling against her skin when he slowed, and she writhed for more.

"Don't tease me…" she panted out.

But that's exactly what he was going to do. He kissed the inside of one thigh and then turned his head to kiss the other. She quivered. "*Diego.*"

The breathless demand in her voice along with ten fingernails digging into his shoulders made him smile.

"You'd laugh at me after getting me to this…this *state*?"

He lowered his head and took a leisurely lick at her.

Her eyes practically rolled back in her head as she rocked up into his mouth, her fingers fisted in his hair now. She was probably going to make him bald before he hit thirty-one, but he didn't care. Instead, he did it again, and she cried out. So, he repeated it. Over and over until she came for him, her body damp and trembling as he reached for his nightstand and grabbed a condom.

She sat up and insisted on rolling it on, which had *him* sweating because her hands felt so good. And the way she'd gotten up close and personal on her knees, the tip of her tongue out as she concentrated, he had to close his eyes to try and avoid finishing before he'd even barely gotten started.

He slowly pushed into her, stopping immediately when her nails dug into his ass. He didn't want to hurt her, he never wanted to hurt her.

"Oh my God, don't stop." Her voice was soft and throaty. "Please, don't stop."

"I'm not hurting you?"

"No!" She made a little movement with her hips, making him lose what little restraint he had. He sank into her completely. She wrapped her legs around him, holding him as close as she possibly could, her hands roaming his shoulders and back, everywhere she could reach.

Her nails dug into his ass, and he didn't care. Lifting his head, he met her gaze.

She smiled.

And, damn, he was a dead man, because he loved her smile. When he began to move, she moaned and rocked in sync with him. In less than a minute, he was breathing in ragged pants. A guy who ran five miles every morning should not be breathless this fast, but it wasn't the exertion.

It was finally being with her again and discovering that their magic still existed. Her fingers slid back up to tangle in his hair, and she pulled him down for another kiss. Her breathing was quick and shallow, her cheeks flushed. When she opened her eyes, he could see they were stormy gray and filled with desire and hunger.

For him.

She was so beautiful, she made his throat hurt.

She kept her eyes open, and they stared at each other as they moved together, her hips rising to meet his thrusts. So beautiful...

And then he couldn't think anymore because she was coming again, gripping him so tightly, he couldn't breathe—not that he needed air when he had her.

Was there a sweeter sound than hearing his name on her lips, knowing that he'd satisfied her?

No.

He buried his face in the curve of her neck as he came, biting his lip to keep from telling her what he wanted so badly to say.

I love you…still, again…always.

* * * *

He had no idea how much later it was when he came awake, violently aroused. The reason for that was slowly lowering herself onto his body. The moan that escaped his lips tugged a whimper from hers. Going from dead-asleep to wide-awake in a single blink, he rolled, tucking Daisy beneath him, his hands tangling with hers, raising them above her head as he filled her inch by delicious inch until it felt like they were one.

Looking into his eyes, she rocked her hips for more. "Hey," she whispered playfully.

With one hard thrust, he proved that he wasn't feeling playful. But he was most definitely feeling something because he held her to him and growled out, "Hey yourself," before letting her take him places he'd never been with anyone but her.

They fell asleep again, entangled, hearts thumping against each other's chests. The next time Diego woke was different than the time before. Very different.

Because he was alone.

He stared up at the ceiling, replaying the night before in his head. On repeat. He had no idea what any of it meant, except that if he was being honest with himself, nothing had felt so right as being wrapped up in Daisy's arms again. It was if he belonged there.

His cell vibrated across his nightstand, and he glanced over at it.

Rocco.

With a deep breath, he answered. "Hey."

"It's Tyler. I'm sorry, I didn't have your number so I borrowed Rocco's phone."

What Diego knew about Tyler had come mostly from Instagram. The guy was an interior decorator, loved cats and traveling and...Rocco. Which, no matter how complicated Diego's feelings for Daisy were, what he'd seen of Tyler was enough for Diego to like him.

"I know this is probably odd for you," Tyler said into the silence.

"Getting a phone call?"

"Talking to the man who's going to marry your brother."

Diego let out a low laugh and scrubbed a hand down his face. "One of the few things that isn't odd at all, actually. What's up?"

"I'm hoping to talk you into forgiving Rocco. He's been anxious about this, about seeing you again, and I'd like to see him be able to enjoy this week for what it is. His wedding. His *only* wedding."

Tyler's tone was light, easy. Casual. But there was an undertone of protection. For Rocco.

And that, more than anything else, reached Diego. "I can appreciate that. But this thing between Rocco and I...it goes back a whole hell of a long time. You know that."

"I do know that," Tyler said. "I lost my own brother last year."

That single sentence, uttered so quietly, was like a punch to the throat. Diego sat up in bed. "I'm...Christ. Sorry doesn't cover it."

"I know. And thank you," Tyler said. "He was a bit of a dick, but he was my brother. And I'd do anything, *anything* to have Ian at this wedding stuff. That isn't going to happen."

"Are you saying that this dick is alive and therefore should get himself an attitude adjustment?" Diego asked with a small smile.

"I try very hard not to tell heteros what to do. They don't seem to appreciate it."

Diego had to laugh. Hell if he didn't admire the guy. "Noted."

Chapter 6

Daisy was ten minutes late to work, and she had no one to blame but herself—and the fact that she'd had an unintended sleepover.

Wherein there'd not been a lot of actual sleeping.

Just the thought gave her a body shiver of the very best kind as she rushed into the office wearing yesterday's clothes and possibly a well-satisfied smile. She'd noticed it while trying to wrangle her hair into a knot on top of her head, but she hadn't been able to get rid of the expression.

A side effect of man-made orgasms that she'd nearly forgotten about.

She rushed directly into a meeting that had already started, ignoring the long, unhappy gaze Carol sent her. After the meeting, in which they'd discussed an upcoming charity event at the opera house ad nauseam while Daisy did her best to stay awake, Carol asked her to hang back.

When it was just the two of them in the conference room, Carol's brows rose.

"What?"

"You were late."

"Ten minutes, yes," Daisy said. "I'm terribly sorry, but it was a first-time offense that won't happen again."

"See that it doesn't." Carol got to her feet. "And you do realize you're wearing yesterday's clothes."

If Carol had been hoping for an explanation, she wasn't going to get one.

When Daisy remained mute regarding the comment, Carol shook her head. "The future head of this company doesn't do walks of shame into morning meetings. Am I clear?"

"I'm not doing a walk of shame," Daisy said. And she meant it. She didn't consider her sex life shameful. Nor was it up for public consumption. "Now, if you'll excuse me, as you know, I've got a lot on my plate."

* * * *

That night, Daisy was at home, once again in PJs and eating ice cream straight from the tub when there came a knock at her door.

She froze, wooden spoon loaded and halfway to her mouth because she didn't have to wonder who was on the other side. Her suddenly perky nipples told her.

Damn. Why had she already showered and removed her armor-slash-mascara? Why was she wearing Hello Kitty PJs? Why couldn't she be in her Wonder Woman set?

Daisy remained still for a moment, waiting to see if maybe he'd go away, so she didn't have to face last night's stupid transgression.

He knocked again. Dammit. He wasn't going away. Daisy sucked down the ice cream on her spoon before heading to the door, half of her brain trying to find ways to delay, the other half trying to make her legs move faster.

When she opened up, she expected a smile at her appearance. Or some smartass remark.

Instead, Diego met her gaze. "What happened to us?" he asked quietly.

The sentence shocked her and gave her heart an odd kick.

"Um…we got naked to some hopefully mutual satisfaction. The end."

"Definitely mutual satisfaction," he said without a smile. "But I'm not talking about last night, and you know that."

She drew in a deep breath. "Then that's a far more difficult question than I'm equipped to handle right now."

"You going to let me in?"

She moved aside. When he caught sight of the open container of ice cream, the corners of his mouth twitched. "Rocky road?"

His favorite, too. Daisy gestured to it, and he made himself at home on the couch, patting the spot next to him.

She hesitated. Not because she didn't want Diego. She did. She wanted him badly. But she also knew what a terrible idea it would be to give in to temptation again. She could fall for him, hard.

Hell, she already had. A decade ago, and nothing had changed. But she could at least try to avoid getting hurt again.

He cocked his head. "Problem?"

"I'm trying to decide if I can trust myself to sit next to you."

He nodded as if he understood. "Which way are you leaning?"

"Towards running for the hills."

An almost-smile appeared. "I won't bite. Unless you ask real nice."

"It's not you I'm worried about," she muttered, making him laugh.

Ignoring the way the sound scraped at her good spots, she sat, making sure not to touch him. Because if she did, she knew herself. Once she felt the heat and strength of him, her brain would shut off, and her body would take over. But that wasn't going to happen tonight. Or any night. It couldn't, or she'd fall hard for him again and not be able to get up.

She expected him to devour the ice cream like in the old days. Back then, date night had sometimes been watching TV and eating ice cream on the couch—and then ignoring the TV and ice cream…

Diego turned to face her. She could feel the weight of his gaze, and she held her breath. *Don't ask me again...*

"What happened to us? What went wrong?"

Damn. She sighed. "Diego, you know."

"What I know is that you went to New York for that scholarship when you could have stayed and accepted your other offer right here in San Francisco."

Daisy did her best to temper herself. He knew she'd grown up rough, always needing to have her own back. Leaving had been her one chance to get out of the gutter, and yeah, she'd taken it. But...she'd also regretted it.

With twenty-twenty hindsight being what it was, she now knew that she'd taken that offer rather than let her biggest fear come true—that she'd never make anything of herself. That she'd end up just like her mom, living off welfare and just barely getting by. "The San Francisco offer didn't come with a full ride. I couldn't afford that option."

"We'd have found a way."

She gave him a get-real look. "Really? Because when I tried to talk to you about it, you just said, 'You gotta do what's best for you.'"

"Daisy—"

"Look, I get it," she said. "Your dad had just had a stroke, and Rocco bailed on you, leaving you the tattoo shop, the house, and your dad's recovery to deal with. All of it on your shoulders. I also get that you had to give up your college experience at Cal. I never blamed you for resenting *me* for going to New York—"

"That wasn't it," Diego said tightly. "Jesus." He shoved his fingers into his hair. "Do you really think I resented you for getting something you wanted so badly?"

She stared up into his unhappy face and let out a breath. "No. That wasn't very kind of me to say. I know you didn't resent me. I know you were overwhelmed. But you shut me out, Diego. I offered to help, I tried to help, but you always pushed me away, saying you had it."

"Because if I couldn't have *my* dreams of getting out," he said, "I wanted you to have yours. And I knew that wasn't staying and watching me go down in flames. But you faded away from me."

The reality was that she'd left thinking that they could still make it work, but whenever she tried to stay in contact, he'd been unwilling to communicate. Their calls had slowly gotten further and further apart. And she'd felt for him because he'd been in a really bad spot. But she'd wanted to be important to him. She'd *needed* to be important to someone, anyone, but especially to him.

"Daisy," he said, his voice low with frustration. "You don't have to temper yourself, not with me, never with me. Just tell me what you're thinking."

"All right." She met his gaze. "You were important to me," she said. "But I didn't feel important to you."

He looked stunned. "You were the most important thing in my life."

"Really? Because when I left here for school, my life fell apart. My housing fell through, and so did a good portion of my funding. I was eating ramen and peanut butter. You didn't even realize I was couch surfing. I got what you were facing, but all I needed was for you to ask how I was."

"God." He drew in a breath. "I'm sorry, Daisy. I hate that you were living like that, but I didn't realize. I was—"

"Busy. Swamped, really, and probably drowning, I know." She softened her voice. "And I get it. You were eighteen years old and all by yourself when it came to your dad's care, the tattoo shop, the house…everything. I hated that Rocco took off on you guys the way he did. You had to give up school and your entire life to take care of everything."

Diego was quiet for a long moment, reflective. "When you left," he finally said quietly, "I was…" He shook his head. "Devastated."

"I was too. But, Diego, you checked out of our relationship way before I called it off. I felt like I was working really hard to be in a relationship with a man I loved so much but who didn't have time for me. And I promised myself I wasn't going to live my life being second best to the people I cared about. Not ever again."

He looked stunned. "I..." He shook his head, looking uncharacteristically unsure. "I had no idea. What you're describing, what I did to you, checking out like that, it's exactly what Rocco did to me. He didn't have time for me, not to help or be around, and I..." He shook his head again. "And I've hated him for it all this time. And yet I did the exact same thing to you."

She could see the pain and regret in his eyes and felt her own fill. "Diego—"

"I'm sorry, Daisy," he said with quiet steel, so genuinely and honestly that her throat tightened.

"I know," she said softly. "I know it wasn't personal. You were so young. Just a kid really, burdened with so much. Looking back, I can't believe you handled it all with as much grace as you did, but..."

"But what?" he asked, moving closer to her, sliding his big, warm hands to her hips.

"But you need to go."

He blinked, clearly unprepared for that.

"You have to," she managed. "If you stay, if we keep spending time like this, I'll fall again. And I can't. I just can't go through it again. Nothing can happen tonight that I'll regret."

Diego stilled, then with a finger under her chin, tipped her face to his. "I hear you, but you're crying..." He gently swiped away the few tears she hadn't even realized she'd shed. "I can't walk away while you're upset."

With a sigh, she sank into him, pressing her face to his throat.

"Let me be here for you like I should have been all those years ago," he said quietly, gathering her in. "Nothing's going to happen, just me holding you."

She laughed and cried at the same time. "We were never any good with just holding each other."

"Trust me," he murmured, slowly wrapping her up against his chest in a warm, full-body hug that had her closing her eyes and burrowing into him, taking comfort from a source she hadn't seen coming. But *everything* about him was comforting, always had been. Like mac and cheese. Like ice cream. And he smelled good. So damn good. Pressing her face to the crook of his neck, she just breathed him in. And, somehow, the fingers of one hand found their way into his hair as she cuddled into his side, her other hand sliding across his abs.

How many nights had they sat just like this, watching movies, talking, laughing...making love? She closed her eyes at the thought, the scruff of his jaw rough against her face—which she loved.

Then she felt him swallow hard and pull back to stand.

"What are you doing?"

"I said you could trust me not to let anything happen. To make that true, I've got to go."

His hair was tousled from her fingers, his shirt untucked, the fit of his jeans making it clear that leaving was the last thing his body wanted to do.

And yet he was going to walk away. Because she'd asked him to. "Diego."

His dark, heated eyes met hers and softened. "Yeah?"

"Don't go."

He held her gaze for a beat and then slowly shook his head. "I promised you," he said gruffly. "And I'm not going to ever break a promise to you again." And then he was gone.

Chapter 7

Diego drove straight to Rocco's house. The whole way over there, his sudden epiphany bounced around in his head like a ping-pong ball. Daisy had clearly spent a lot of years resenting him for what he'd done, for how he'd shut her out, closed himself off to what was happening in her life. But at the time, his life had been a chaotic disaster.

When Rocco did the same to him, Diego had hated him for it. He'd nursed a grudge for a decade now, and though he liked to pride himself on being a stand-up guy, a good man, the truth was that he hadn't always been.

Rocco was currently living in their childhood home with Tyler. There were a lot of memories associated with the place, and it seemed like every single one of them were pummeling Diego as he walked up the path.

The last time he'd been here had been the day of his dad's funeral. After, he'd packed to leave and never came back. He'd stood on this very walkway, a duffle bag over one shoulder, facing off with Rocco, who hadn't wanted him to go.

Ironic, since after their dad's stroke two years before that, Rocco had taken off for the Caribbean to blow off steam.

And he'd stayed gone until that day.

For Diego, it'd been too much. His dad was gone, and so was

he.

Rocco opened the door to his knock, and for a moment, Diego couldn't tell the past from the here and now.

Tyler came up behind Rocco, a hand on his fiancé's shoulder whether in solidarity or restraint, Diego didn't know. Diego met Tyler's eyes. At whatever the man saw there, he nodded, squeezed Rocco's shoulder, and then left the brothers alone.

"Hey," Rocco said, clearly stunned to see him. "Uh…everything okay?"

"Yeah." Diego shook his head. "No. Listen…I just wanted you to know that I get it now. If I'd had a chance to be with someone I was in love with in the Caribbean, I'd have stayed gone, too."

Rocco blinked and scrubbed a hand over the top of his head in a move that Diego recognized as one his father used to do all the time when he didn't know what to say. Even as he thought it, Diego caught himself doing the same thing and stopped.

But not before Rocco gave him a small, wry smile. "Apple and tree and all that."

"Yeah."

"You going to invite him in?" Tyler called from somewhere in the house. "Or stand there staring at each other like a pair of idiots?"

Another flash of a wry smile from Rocco, who backed up to let Diego in.

They ended up in the kitchen at the table where Diego had spent years doing homework, eating them out of house and home, and learning to cook so they didn't starve. The electric outlet by the toaster on the counter still had black smudge marks from the time he'd almost burned the house down making grilled cheese.

Tyler served them tea and then gave them both a kiss on top of their heads before he left the room.

"He means well," Rocco said but rose. He pulled a bottle of brandy from a cupboard and dumped a liberal amount into both teas.

They sat across the table from each other, awkward. Silent. Tense.

"I came to apologize," Diego said. For all those years of silence and resentment and—"

"Don't. Don't apologize, not to me." Rocco pushed his untouched tea aside and took a swig straight from the brandy bottle. "I don't deserve it. We both know I don't. I deserted you, Diego."

Diego drew in a deep breath. "Yeah. But after talking to Daisy, I realized I did the same thing to her that you did to me. And I had my reasons for it. They were even good ones. But I don't want to be that guy. I'm sorry I was that guy."

Rocco's breath came out in a whoosh. "And I'm sorry I was a selfish dick. The fact that I always have been, isn't an excuse, I know. But I regret like hell what I did." He paused for another moment. When he finally went on, his voice was thick with emotion. "I've missed you, man."

The words washed over Diego like a healing balm, and he nodded. "Missed you, too."

Rocco stood and hauled Diego out of his chair as if he didn't weigh anything and pulled him in for a bear hug. After a long moment, Rocco pushed back. "Wait a minute. If you just had that conversation with Daisy, then why the hell are you here with me? Why aren't you guys making up for lost time?"

Diego shook his head and turned away.

"What does that mean?" Rocco asked Diego's back. "I saw how you two looked at each other."

"We're not going there. I'm leaving right after the wedding."

Rocco turned him around and stared at him as if Diego had lost his mind. "You can't be serious."

"Of course, I'm serious. I don't live here anymore. I live in San Diego, where I've got a great job being in charge of a fleet of tourist boats. I also work once a week at a tattoo shop for a buddy of mine, so I get that fix, too. Everything's good down there for me." Or it had been until he'd come back here and realized how little he actually felt anymore—about *anything*. He'd felt more in the past few days here than he had in years.

Rocco's expression said that he called bullshit. His words proved it. "Let me give you three reasons why you should stay," he said tightly. "One, you should be tattooing for *our* family legacy, at The Canvas Shop. I miss you there, big time. And you could be working at the marina here in San Fran, as well. You remember Jake?"

"Of course." Diego and Rocco had gone to school with Jake, who'd gone straight into the military after graduation and had come home a paraplegic. He now owned and operated a fleet of tourist boats near Pier 39.

"He'd hire you in a hot minute to do what you're already doing for someone else."

"I like San Diego."

"Which brings me to points two and three," Rocco said. "San Diego doesn't have me. And even more importantly, San Diego doesn't have Daisy."

Diego shook his head. "It's not that easy, Rocco."

"Again, bullshit."

* * * *

Back on his boat late that night, Diego had to shake his head. He'd somehow been talked into hanging out at the tattoo shop the next day before his next wedding task, which was picking the wedding band from the final five. Because according to Rocco, if he let Tyler do it, a decision would never get made. Diego's head was spinning, and he had to keep repeating the words he'd given Rocco—*it's not that easy…*

But then he thought about how it'd felt to be with his brother again, how much he liked seeing how happy he was with Tyler, and how it would feel to have them back in his life.

Then he thought about Daisy, and how right it'd felt with her the other night. And not even just in bed, but out of it, too. Talking. Laughing. Just being… It'd all felt shockingly right.

It's not that easy…

Nothing ever was, not in his experiences.

But maybe…just *maybe* this time it could be.

* * * *

The next evening, he was just getting off his bike in front of Daisy's place when she stepped outside in a long-sleeved knit dress that clung to her curves in a way that made his mouth water. Or maybe that was her knee-high black leather boots. She was shrugging into a leather jacket when she saw him and froze.

"What are you doing?" she asked. "I assumed we were meeting at the first venue." She had a list in her hand and looked at it. "The band's going on in thirty minutes."

"Yes," he said. "I got the same list. But mine says to pick you up."

They stared at each other.

"You know," she said slowly. "I'm starting to smell a rat."

"Two of them."

She pulled out her phone and hit a number. She put it on speaker and tapped her toes impatiently. "Hey," she said when Rocco answered. "Why didn't you tell me you were having Diego pick me up?"

"I'm sure I mentioned it," Rocco said.

"You didn't."

"Huh. Sorry, honey. Wedding brain. I can't keep a thought in my head. Is there a problem?"

Daisy looked up into Diego's eyes. Once upon a time, he'd been able to read her like a book, and the skill was coming back to him. Like getting on a bike. She was thinking, yeah, she had a problem, and its name was Diego. He smiled.

She rolled her eyes. "No problem," she told Rocco and disconnected. "Let's get this over with."

The first venue was a restaurant and bar on the wharf, with a deck that was suspended over the water. It was packed. The band was playing top hits from the '80s, and they were good enough that when Daisy started moving to the beat with a tantalizing, hopeful smile, Diego took her hand and led her out to the dance floor.

As he remembered all too well, she could move. And watching her lose herself in the fun and the music loosened him up in a way that he hadn't felt in a long time. It made him feel like he'd been drinking. Unable to resist, he tugged her to him when a slow song came on, and they moved together as one.

"Miss this," he murmured against her ear, the words escaping without conscious thought.

"San Francisco?"

"You."

She stared up at him with those big eyes.

"You don't believe me?"

"I'd like to think you missed me," she said. "As much as you'd miss, say, a limb."

He smiled. "How do you know I didn't?"

Biting her lower lip, she rolled her eyes, whether at herself or him, he had no idea. "I know."

His smile vanished. "You're wrong. I missed you more than I'd miss a limb. I missed you with my entire being."

"I missed you, too," she finally whispered. "Even when I was still angry and hurt, I missed you." She hesitated. "A lot."

"Daisy…" Pulling her in a little tighter, he ran a hand up her spine and into her hair, wrecked at the thought of how much he'd hurt her. "I'm so sorry. I never meant to desert you. I had no idea—"

She put a finger over his lips. "We talked it out. I get it. It's okay, you don't have to apologize again. I mean…" Her tone lightened. "Unless you do something else stupid enough to warrant an apology."

Warmth filled a hole in his chest that he didn't even realize he had. "I don't plan on it."

"Good to know."

He held her close through the slow song. "Rocco and I talked."

Daisy looked up at him in surprise, clearly hopeful that he and his brother had worked things out, which touched him in ways he hadn't known he could be touched.

He nodded. "We're going to be okay." He paused. "He wants me to stay in San Francisco and help him run The Canvas Shop. I could also get a job with Jake at the marina."

Her gaze briefly skittered away. "Is that something you'd want to do? Stay?"

"Would *you* want me to?" he asked and found himself holding his breath.

She stared at him for a long beat, her eyes saying yes, which had him breathing again. Until she spoke, her tone not matching her eyes. "That's…a lot of pressure," she said quietly. "I'd never ask anyone to move because of me."

Not what he'd wanted to hear, but what had he expected? He'd hurt her, she wouldn't want to take another chance on him.

When the song ended, he lowered his head and kissed her without thought. It was simply like drawing in air. When she moaned and pressed closer, he deepened the embrace, not breaking away until the music revved up again and they were bumped from all sides by people dancing.

"We should get going," she said. "To check out the next band."

Right. The next venue was another restaurant and bar in the Castro district. They walked up the rainbow-colored sidewalks and into the place that smelled so delicious they ordered food.

Over a pile of hors d'oeuvres, they dug in. Diego worked his way through a stack of wings and pizza chips and was headed for the *queso* when Daisy spoke and had him stilling.

"This is nice."

"It is," he said. "But last night you were reluctant to go there with me again."

"I know. I know I must seem like an emotional see-saw, and I don't mean to be making you dizzy with it. I just couldn't see how this could ever work out between us."

"And…something changed that?" he asked and then held his breath.

"I decided I would regret not even being willing to try."

Her words both revved him up and also calmed his heart. "Me, too," he said quietly.

She was playing with the condensation on her glass. When he'd picked her up earlier, she'd had that polished, professional, can't-touch-this look about her, and that had been hot as hell.

But she'd been dancing and had imbibed a bit. She was flushed. She'd let her hair down, and it was wild around her face. She stared at his mouth in a way that made him want to do a whole bunch of really wicked things to her.

This band was even better than the first, and Daisy looked happy and relaxed and sexy as hell, and Diego had no idea how he was going to let her walk away from him again.

"Dance with me," she demanded softly, letting her gaze travel the length of him. At whatever she saw, she smiled and stood. Then she pulled him up, and with her hands on his chest, shimmied close to him.

She was going to be the death of him.

But he let her draw him out onto the dance floor, where she slowly slid her hands up his biceps and wound her arms around his neck, all while wriggling the sexy, hot bod that fulfilled his every fantasy. With a low groan, he yanked her roughly into him and let his fingers slowly trail down her back, his hand cupping her ass to press her closer.

With a gasp, she met his gaze. "You want me," she breathed.

"Yeah, but what I want, I can't have. At least not on this dance floor."

She bit her lower lip and kept moving against him, practically glowing as if it were her greatest wish to drive him as insane with lust as he could possibly get.

Mission accomplished.

But two could play this game. Eyes locked, he dragged his hand up from the curve of her ass, his fingers scoring lightly up her back to tangle in her hair. With a gentle tug, her throat was exposed, and his mouth instantly covered the curve between her shoulder and neck. His other hand rested lightly on her hip as he started moving slowly in time with the driving bass of the music.

She moaned low in her throat and closed her eyes. The lights above them blinked and changed color to the beat of the band. Diego couldn't have said what the song was, whether it was fast or slow. He couldn't have said how many people were on the dance floor. Hell, he couldn't recall his own full name. Because when she looked at him like she was, her eyes hot and dark, he could think of nothing at all.

"Diego?" she whispered.

"Yeah, babe?"

"Take me home."

He couldn't get her out of there fast enough, grabbing her hand, tugging her toward the dimly lit exit. Snippets of muffled conversations reached him, the vibrations of the music as they exited out into the night.

"Your place or the boat?" he asked when he had them on the road.

"Most definitely the boat," Daisy said in his ear, a move that gave him the very best kind of shiver down his spine.

Twenty minutes later, they were walking down the marina dock towards his vessel. He was holding her hand because though the docks were lit, it was still tricky going at night. His body was on high alert, feeling tight and achy and anticipatory.

Given the way Daisy was breathing, she felt the same.

She stopped walking and turned to him. "Diego?"

"Yeah?"

"I lied before."

He stilled. "When?"

"When you asked me if I wanted you to stay, and I said that it was too much pressure. That was the lie. I want you to stay."

Chapter 8

Daisy had to practically run to keep up with Diego's long-legged stride down the dock. She laughed breathlessly. "In a hurry?"

Since his answer was a low, nearly inaudible growl, she went from amused to almost having an orgasm in zero point four seconds. At his boat, he physically lifted her up and in, following so closely they were touching the whole time.

"On the top deck?" she asked hopefully, thinking about how it might feel to be pinned beneath him, the stars above, the sounds of the water surge slapping up against the boat...

"No," he said. "Below deck." He had a grip on her, tugging her to the stairs.

"But—"

He guided her down, then pressed her up against the door without turning on a light. "Another time beneath the stars," he promised. "Tonight, I have plans."

"Plans?"

"Yes, and they involve making you cry out my name over and over again. And call me selfish, but that...that sound from your lips, Daisy, is for me alone."

Her bones liquified. But that was okay because Diego had her.

He had her against the door, held there by his big body while shutting out the rest of the world. She felt him nibble her throat and had to laugh breathlessly. She was already halfway to crying out his name.

Then his hands were in her hair, his mouth on hers, not a single space between them. His body was deliciously hard. Everywhere.

Then, suddenly, he pulled back from her. Without notice, she was alone. She opened her eyes, but she couldn't see a damn thing, not even a faint outline of him. The only light came from a narrow line of moonlight slanting vertically down the middle of the bed and the floor, ending at her feet. "Diego?"

He stepped into the shaft of moonlight. Wordlessly, he tugged his shirt over his head and dropped it on the floor.

He was gorgeous bathed in the glow, his lean, tough muscles rippling with his every movement, his body reminding her of a sleek, powerful cat. A wild one.

She heard the dull thud of his boots hitting the floor. The rest of his clothes followed, and he turned to her, making her swallow hard.

Mine, she thought.

"Now you," he said. But before Daisy could, he came to her and turned her away from him, placing her hands on the wall. He slowly unzipped her dress, nudging it off her shoulders and past her hips before leaning his body into hers and pressing his mouth to her shoulder. Her bra fell away like magic as he kissed and nibbled his way to the crook of her neck, the column of her throat, and then he was at her ear. "I can't wait to be inside you again," he said. "The way you pant my name drives me insane."

It was a good thing he was holding her up. But then he wasn't. He'd dropped to his knees to unzip and pull off her boots. Then her tights. When his fingers hooked in her undies, she made a sound, and then another when he slid them down.

"I...can't stand," she managed.

Far more adaptable in any given situation than she was, he rose to his feet and took her with him to the bed. She hit the mattress on her back, and he followed her down. Their gazes met and locked, and in his eyes, she saw the things that hopes and dreams were made of. Her heart rate spiked. Feeling emotionally exposed, she actually tried to look away until she realized that the vulnerability she saw reflected back wasn't hers, but *his*.

Cupping his jaw, she whispered his name, and then he was inside her. Their bodies moved together as if they'd been built for each other, hips surging and retreating in sync. She never wanted this to end. His weight holding her down, how he looked at her when he brushed the hair from her face, his hand reaching for and gripping hers tightly on the pillow beside her head. It all combined as wordless pleas and demands that tumbled from her lips.

"I've got you," he said. "I promise."

The sweet words uttered so roughly cascaded through her. Arching up, she came, shuddering into him. Somehow, she managed to open her eyes because she didn't want to miss a single second.

His head was back, the cords of his neck taut, his entire body strung tightly, his hands gripping hers hard as he finally let himself come, her name on his lips.

* * * *

Diego came awake the next morning to find Daisy sprawled across him, one leg thrown over his, her arm heavy across his abs, a hand gripping his biceps, face pressed into his chest. Her hair was all up in his face, and he was pretty sure she was drooling on him a little bit.

Carefully, he slid out from under her. Still deeply asleep, she murmured her displeasure and snuggled into the spot he'd vacated, never waking up.

He had a ridiculously primal response, knowing that he'd put her into a near coma. With a smile he couldn't tame, he made coffee and whipped up some bacon and eggs. Breakfast of champions.

Daisy still hadn't so much as budged by the time he finished, so he leaned against the counter and drank his coffee, content to just watch her sleep.

On the counter at his side, her smartphone screen lit up as an email came in. Another guy, a better guy, would've probably looked away. And Diego started to, but the subject line caught his eye: *Daisy's and Poppy's Grand NYC Venture.*

And…because of the way she had her settings, he could see the first two lines of the email.

Hey hon! I put together the budget we talked about for the new business AND I found a few places right here in NYC that are actually available and almost, sort of, in our budget. Both attached, hurry up and move back!

Diego had to set his mug of hot coffee down before he dropped it. Her phone went dark, but he didn't need to see the email again. Last night, she'd said things. Like the soft, sweetly uttered, "I missed you…" and, "I want you to stay…"

What the hell had that been about if she'd known she was moving back to New York?

It was such a terrible, awful instant replay of what had happened the first time they'd been together. Once again, he'd fallen in love with her. And once again, it'd thrown his world into turmoil. Love always did. It took all the power from him and gave it to someone whose decisions could affect his life in a negative way. Like his dad. Like Rocco. Like Daisy—for the second time.

Apparently, he was a slow learner, but he finally got it. He was done with this. Done with love.

Chapter 9

Daisy woke to the scent of coffee. Not yet opening her eyes, she smiled and stretched, reaching out for Diego, but he wasn't in bed, and the sheets were cool on his side.

This had her opening her eyes and sitting up.

Diego was across the room in the galley area, leaning back against the counter, sipping at a mug of coffee.

Watching her.

He wore his jeans unfastened and nothing else, which meant they sat dangerously low on his hips. His hair was uncombed, his jaw unshaven, his bare feet crossed.

The wild mountain cat playing at domesticity.

She pushed the hair from her face, and even though the sheet covered her, she felt self-conscious. Which was silly, given that he'd seen everything she had. Seen. Touched. Kissed. Nibbled… "Hey."

"Hey." He set his mug aside and said nothing more.

She wondered how to get out of bed without revealing just how naked she felt. She tried wrapping herself up the best she could and stood. But when she took a step, the sheet—still tucked in at the foot of the bed—deserted her.

Instead of teasing her or enjoying the view, he tossed her his shirt from the back of a chair.

She quickly pulled it down over her head, thankful that it fell to her mid-thighs. "So…" she said. "Good morning."

He poured coffee into a second mug and handed it to her. "I don't know about good."

Yeah, something was very off. Her stomach clenched. Last night had been good. No, correction, it had been amazing. So, what had gone wrong between then and now?

"You got an email," he said. "Someone named Poppy has the numbers on the new business and the perfect apartment for you." He paused. "In New York."

Oh. Oh, shit. "I meant to tell you about that."

"Before or after you said you wanted me to move back home?"

"Poppy's my old college roommate," she said. "And, yeah, we talked about starting up our own event company. The deal was that we each come up with a proposal for our prospective cities and then talk. I didn't commit to going to New York."

"But you thought about it."

"I did," she admitted. "But that doesn't mean I'm going."

Diego turned away. "You've got to do whatever you've got to do. Same for me. I'll be heading out of here right after the wedding."

She ignored the way his dismissive tone sliced right through her. Or tried to. But it was impossible to do so because, in spite of their off-the-charts chemistry in bed, he was once again not putting her first. "So, you saw an email, and just like that, you're ready to bail," she said. "Again. Do I have that right?"

"Actually, the first time, *you* bailed."

"No, Diego," she said, voice tight with anger and frustration. And sadness. Damn, so much sadness. *"You* did. In fact, you've had one foot out the door since the beginning, even when just last night you let me think this was going somewhere."

His expression was closed-off, eyes hooded, jaw set, mouth grim. "We're not going to have a long-distance relationship and let it fade away like it did before," he said.

"Well, you're right about that. We're absolutely not going to have a relationship," Daisy said, looking for her clothes, which were still on the floor. Damn. Hard to be righteous and strong when you had to bend over wearing nothing but a man's t-shirt to pick up the clothes you'd strewn to Hell and back the night before. "And just FYI, back then, nothing faded away," she said tightly, pulling on her tights. "*You* checked out."

"I apologized for that," Diego said, his voice low and rigid. "And I meant it. I screwed up, and I know it. But I thought we had something, something good that we were going to work for."

"So did I," she said. "Did you ever stop to think that maybe the reason I hadn't told you about the NYC thing is because I wasn't going to go?"

When he just looked at her, she shook her head. "Good to know that you've got faith in me. I'm not doing this with you again, Diego. This is more than a stupid misunderstanding. This is mistrust, a deep mistrust right at your core. And I can't fix that. I can't change that. And I won't live with it, not ever again." She was trying not to cry, giving up on figuring out how to get her bra on beneath his shirt, which she wasn't going to take off. Yep, she was going to Lyft home in a man's thankfully very long t-shirt, tights, and boots.

As soon as she got in the last word. "Last night, you let me think that you relocating here might be for me, but that clearly wasn't true. If you're trying to get me to understand that I'm not now—nor will I ever be—your first choice, message received." She stopped to realize that she'd just picked up his socks, not hers, and threw them at him. They may or may not have hit him in the face. She zipped up her boots and turned in a circle, grabbing her remaining items. Her dress. Her bra. Her purse.

"Daisy—"

"No," she said, snatching her phone from the counter and opening her Lyft app. "If I was really important to you, you'd say, 'hey, you know what? We'll make this work no matter what. And hell, I can even come to New York if that's what you need to do.'"

Diego suddenly seemed just as angry as she was. Actually, she could have sworn that she saw a flash of something else in his dark gaze. Fear. But it was gone in a blink. "The only person in that scenario giving anything up is me," he said. "And I'm done with giving up everything for the people in my life."

Something in the way he'd worded that had her stop, checking herself. Then she realized...it was the same way he'd described having to come home after only a semester of college when he'd had to drop everything—his entire life—to come back and take care of his dad. "Diego," she said, her voice softer. "I'm not asking anything of you. I don't want anything that you don't freely give."

His expression didn't budge, and with a shake of her head, she started to walk out. But she stopped and met his gaze one last time. "I want you to know that I really wasn't keeping the new business plans from you. I'd already decided I wanted to stay here, in the city. Good luck in San Diego."

"When did you make that decision?" he asked.

"Not that it matters, but I decided the night you came to my house and asked me what happened between us. And you know what? If back when your dad had gotten sick, you'd wanted me to stay with you, I would have. I'd have given up everything to be with you. I even asked if I could, and you said no. You had to bear the burden alone. You never asked me to stay. And now I know why. Because if you had, you couldn't be the martyr right now, standing there all righteous and blaming me for all of this." And with that, she walked out.

Daisy exited the boat and strode up the docks, getting a text that her Lyft was pulling into the lot. The only thing to go right so far.

Chapter 10

Diego couldn't have said what he did with the day. It was just getting dark when he once again found himself standing outside Rocco's door. When his brother opened up, he looked surprised before sliding a look past Diego, clearly looking for something.

"What?" Diego asked.

"Where's Daisy?"

Already on shaky ground and not really sure why he was there, Diego shook his head. "I don't know."

"Okay. It's only the eve of my wedding, and you've lost my wedding planner. No big deal." Rocco met his gaze. "Why do you look like someone just died?"

"Babe, don't badger him on the doorstep," Tyler said, coming up behind Rocco. "You invite him in so we can badger him with some privacy."

They led Diego to the kitchen where Tyler had a full spread of food going. He piled a plate sky-high and handed it to Diego, who shook his head. "No thanks."

"Shit," Rocco said, taking the plate meant for Diego. "If he's not hungry, something's really wrong. What did you do?"

Diego blew out a breath. "Pissed her off."

"You could do that by breathing."

Tyler shook his head at Rocco. "Okay, so you pissed her off, and then you...what? Just let her go?" Tyler asked.

"Well, yeah," Diego said. "It's not like I had options. I couldn't make her stay and talk to me."

"Oh, honey," Tyler said in a tone that said he really meant *you're such an idiot* as he shook his head. "I mean, you're right, you can't make a woman do anything she doesn't want to do. Or anyone for that matter. But you could have tried to make her *want* to stay and have it out with you. Women need to feel appreciated and adored." He flashed a quick smile at Rocco. "Well, some men do too, but I'm told it's a non-negotiable requirement for a woman."

"What did you do?" Rocco asked.

"I thought she was going back to New York," Diego said, lifting a shoulder. "Acted like a dick."

Tyler clucked his tongue. "It runs in the family."

"I'd say I'm insulted, but..." Rocco reached out for Tyler's hand. "It's totally true." He met Diego's gaze. "Tell us everything."

"Things were...good," Diego said. "I thought we were going to get together and make it work this time. She asked if I was going to move back here—"

"And?" Rocco asked, leaning forward, eyes sharp. "What did you say?"

Diego shrugged.

"What does that mean?" Rocco asked.

"I said I'd stay...for her."

"But not for me?" Rocco asked.

Tyler gave Rocco a long look.

"Right," Rocco said. "This isn't about me. Go on."

"This morning, I saw an incoming email of hers," Diego said. "About a job and an apartment waiting for her in New York."

"Don't tell me," Tyler said. "You pulled the asshole card and made assumptions."

Diego didn't answer. He didn't have to. He was sure the answer was all over his face.

Rocco shook his head in disgust. "Rookie."

"Hey, you don't get to talk to me about this," Diego said, pointing at him.

Rocco knocked Diego's finger away from his face. "And why the fuck not?"

"Are you kidding me?" Diego asked. "You left me. You fucking flew off to a tropical beach and got laid—" He slid Tyler an apologetic look. "No offense."

"None taken, honey."

Diego nodded and went back to Rocco. "And you never came back."

"I apologized for that," Rocco said quietly, sincerely.

"I know. And I'm over it. I *am*," Diego insisted. "But Dad left me. Mom left me. And I just watched the only woman I've ever loved walk out the door. And I get it. It's not the people in my life. It's me." He stood up.

Rocco did the same, catching his brother at the door, spinning him back to face him, giving him a shake. "It's not you." In a surprise move, he pulled Diego into him for a hard hug. "It's not you," he said again fiercely.

Diego let out a rough breath but found he couldn't draw another one in because of Rocco's grip.

"Babe, please don't accidentally suffocate our best man," Tyler said. "Now, both of you, come back and sit down. Eat."

And what Tyler wanted, Tyler got. They sat. They ate. And after, Diego looked at Rocco. "Tell me."

"Tell you what?" Rocco asked innocently.

"Whatever it is you still haven't told me. It's got to be big, given that you've managed to keep a secret."

"Hey, I can keep a secret."

Both Diego and Tyler laughed.

"Fine," Rocco said. "It's about the prewedding stuff you've been handling for us with Daisy…"

"Yeah? You need something else?"

Tyler put a hand to his heart. "That you'd even ask right now is precious. But, no. We've got a confession." He looked at Rocco.

Who grimaced with…guilt?

"We've been trying to get you and Daisy speaking again," Tyler said. "That's why we kept throwing you two together for all those made-up errands. Because near as we can tell, neither of you have been happy in a long time."

"Made-up errands? You mean the cake tasting, the suit, the bands?"

"Yeah." Rocco blew out a breath. "I made those all up. Did you really think we didn't already have our shit together only a few days before the wedding?"

Diego blinked. "Shit. I don't know, I know zip about weddings." He paused, and his gut tightened. "Was Daisy in on it?"

"No," Rocco said. "She planned a beautiful wedding for us, and then a few months ago, Tyler and I saw an opening, a way to get you home. So, we told her we were scrapping our plans and starting over. We lied to her, saying we were making big, last-minute changes and needed her help."

Diego stared at him and then Tyler, then he looked back at Rocco. "It was all a ruse?"

"Yeah," Rocco said. "And you screwed it up."

Tyler put a hand over Rocco's and gave a small head shake before turning to Diego. "You didn't screw it up. At least, not the wedding. The wedding's all perfectly planned. The Daisy thing, though…"

Diego looked at Rocco. "What the hell were you thinking?"

"I was thinking that she was lonely, and the last person she loved was you. And that I missed you, dammit…"

"He thought he was helping," Tyler said.

Rocco nodded.

This caused a sigh to escape Diego. "You did," he admitted.

Rocco met his gaze, his eyes now having some hope in them.

"Yeah?"

"Yeah." Diego shook his head. "If you hadn't become a meddling, gossiping, nosy body, I'd never have reconnected with her."

The look on Rocco's face was priceless, and Tyler laughed. He laughed so hard he had to sit down. "I'm pretty sure my two-hundred-and-fifty-pound biker badass fiancé has never once in his life been called a meddling, gossiping, nosy body." Tyler swiped tears of mirth from his face. "Priceless."

"It's not fiancé," Rocco muttered. "After tomorrow at our wedding, it's *husband*. I'm going to be your meddling, gossiping, nosy body *husband*."

"And I'm looking forward to it, babe," Tyler said and kissed him.

Diego turned to the door.

"Wait, where are you going?" Rocco asked after breaking off the kiss.

"If *you* can get your life and shit together," Diego said, "then so can I."

He went straight to Daisy's. She wasn't there. She wasn't at her office either. Nor did she answer his embarrassing number of calls and texts. He ended up back at her place and sat outside her door for a few hours before he figured out that she wasn't coming home.

For a minute, he thought maybe he'd chased her right out of town and back to New York, which would suck and suck hard. But he knew she wouldn't go anywhere until after the wedding.

* * * *

Daisy had done what she always did when the going got tough. She buried herself in work. Even though she felt as if she'd been run over by a freight train, she headed to the office. Carol took one look at her and said, "You got dumped."

Daisy supposed Carol must know the feeling in order to

recognize it, but she shrugged. "I'm fine." Actually, she was pissed-off. She'd lost the love of her life for the second time, which was devastating.

But she'd survived before, and she'd survive now.

So, she sucked it up. She reapplied mascara and then went offsite to visit two of Carol's important, high-profile clients, which had thankfully taken her the rest of the day.

The next morning, she woke up knowing that she should be excited about Rocco and Tyler's wedding in a few hours. She lay in bed and tried not to remember how much more fun it was when Diego was in it with her.

And for at least the thousandth time since yesterday, Daisy reminded herself that she was no longer thinking about him.

Except, she was.

A lot.

All the time.

She'd been hasty to run out on him. She knew his past, knew that he had abandonment issues. She could have tried talking to him about things instead of acting like the rash teenager she'd once been.

She showered, dressed, and told herself that the goal for the day was simple: keep herself as busy as possible so she wouldn't have to look at Diego. Shouldn't be a problem with the huge wedding they'd decided upon, in a massive ballroom of their favorite San Fran hotel.

Daisy was just about to leave to get herself to the venue—two hours early to make sure things were playing out as they should—when she got a text from Rocco that said: *change of plans.*

She stared at the message as a new one came in with an address and the following cryptic words: *come here instead.*

Okaaaaay. She tried calling Rocco, but he didn't answer. Nor did Tyler. So, she went to the new address. The Lyft let her off in the beach parking lot.

The. Beach. Parking. Lot.

What the actual hell? Since neither groom was answering his phone, she walked to the lookout and stopped at the top of the stairs.

Below and off to the right in a natural alcove between the water and the rocks stood a wooden archway lined with flowers. In front of it was a small aisle, delineated with stones.

No chairs.

She could see three men. Rocco, Tyler, and Harris, a dear friend of the grooms' who'd married several of their friends. The backdrop was the Golden Gate Bridge, gorgeous enough to steal her breath.

Not understanding—what had happened to the big wedding they said they wanted?—she started to go down the stairs when a hand settled on her arm and gently turned her around.

Diego.

He was in a suit, but in no way had it tamed him. He still looked as wild as ever.

Her heart skipped a beat.

Damn heart.

He spoke first. "It's Rocco and Tyler. It was all a ruse," he said. "To get us back together." He shook his head. "I'm sorry, Daisy. I screwed up. You are the most important thing in my life. You always have been. I just haven't shown you that. Let me show you now. I get that it's probably ten years too late, but I have to try." He gave her a small smile. "I quit my job in San Diego. I've got two choices now. I can go to work for Jake, running and managing his fleet, or I sell my boat and buy a bigger one. In New York."

She gasped. "What?"

"Wherever you land, wherever you decide you want to be, that's where I want to be, as well. Because I pick you. I will always pick you. You have my word on that. I love you, Daisy."

She felt the breath stutter in her chest, and she was pretty sure the bones in her legs had just melted. "I'm not going to New York. Poppy and I are going to start our own company, but we're going the bi-coastal route. Her there, and me here." Daisy drew in a deep breath. "I want to be with you," she said, never having meant anything more. Except for maybe one thing. "I love you too, Diego."

Tyler came jogging up the stairs to them, looking wonderful in his tux. "Oh, baby," he said, looking at Daisy's dress. "It's perfect. I need you to be my bridesmaid."

Rocco was right behind Tyler, looking like he was afraid to be too happy. "And I need my brother at my side. Are we all okay?"

Daisy pulled Rocco in for a hug. "More than. Thank you," she whispered fiercely. "For being such a sneaky bastard."

Rocco kissed her and looked at Diego over her head, clearly needing his brother's reaction.

Diego nodded. "You are a sneaky bastard. But...you're the best sneaky bastard I know. We're also all okay."

Rocco let out a breath, and with suspiciously shiny eyes, turned to Tyler. "Ready to make an honest man out of me?"

Tyler's smile lit up the day around them.

They all headed down to the beach, but Diego pulled Daisy back, waiting until she looked up at him before he cupped her face to look at her very seriously. "I know I've made mistakes. Disappointed you. And I'd like to say I won't ever do it again, but—"

"But you're only human." She smiled. "Neither of us is perfect, Diego. It's a safe bet to say we're both going to make lots more mistakes."

"Maybe, but one I'll never make again is hurting you," Diego said fiercely. "You're it for me, Daisy. You always were." He turned to look at the waiting grooms, the glorious day behind them, and then back at Daisy. "There are times, like now, when all I have to do is look at you..." He sank his fingers into her hair. "And it feels like the only reason my heart is beating in my chest is because yours is beating. The only reason I can breathe is because you're breathing."

She pulled his head down to hers and kissed him softly. "So, let's keep breathing. Together."

"Now there's a pact."

Author's Note

I hope you enjoyed this peek into my Heartbreaker Bay series. I made a quick mention of Sadie and Caleb. Their book is called *Playing For Keeps* and is out now wherever books and ebooks are sold, as well as the rest of the Heartbreaker Bay series, including the latest stand-alone, *Wrapped Up In You.*

Sign up for the 1001 Dark Nights Newsletter
and be entered to win a Tiffany Key necklace.

There's a contest every month!

Go to www.1001DarkNights.com to register.

**As a bonus, all subscribers can download
FIVE FREE exclusive books!**

Discover 1001 Dark Nights Collection Six

Go to www.1001DarkNights.com for more information.

DRAGON CLAIMED by Donna Grant
A Dark Kings Novella

ASHES TO INK by Carrie Ann Ryan
A Montgomery Ink: Colorado Springs Novella

ENSNARED by Elisabeth Naughton
An Eternal Guardians Novella

EVERMORE by Corinne Michaels
A Salvation Series Novella

VENGEANCE by Rebecca Zanetti
A Dark Protectors/Rebels Novella

ELI'S TRIUMPH by Joanna Wylde
A Reapers MC Novella

CIPHER by Larissa Ione
A Demonica Underworld Novella

RESCUING MACIE by Susan Stoker
A Delta Force Heroes Novella

ENCHANTED by Lexi Blake
A Masters and Mercenaries Novella

TAKE THE BRIDE by Carly Phillips
A Knight Brothers Novella

INDULGE ME by J. Kenner
A Stark Ever After Novella

THE KING by Jennifer L. Armentrout
A Wicked Novella

Discover 1001 Dark Nights

Go to www.1001DarkNights.com for more information.

COLLECTION ONE
FOREVER WICKED by Shayla Black
CRIMSON TWILIGHT by Heather Graham
CAPTURED IN SURRENDER by Liliana Hart
SILENT BITE: A SCANGUARDS WEDDING by Tina Folsom
DUNGEON GAMES by Lexi Blake
AZAGOTH by Larissa Ione
NEED YOU NOW by Lisa Renee Jones
SHOW ME, BABY by Cherise Sinclair
ROPED IN by Lorelei James
TEMPTED BY MIDNIGHT by Lara Adrian
THE FLAME by Christopher Rice
CARESS OF DARKNESS by Julie Kenner

COLLECTION TWO
WICKED WOLF by Carrie Ann Ryan
WHEN IRISH EYES ARE HAUNTING by Heather Graham
EASY WITH YOU by Kristen Proby
MASTER OF FREEDOM by Cherise Sinclair
CARESS OF PLEASURE by Julie Kenner
ADORED by Lexi Blake
HADES by Larissa Ione
RAVAGED by Elisabeth Naughton
DREAM OF YOU by Jennifer L. Armentrout
STRIPPED DOWN by Lorelei James
RAGE/KILLIAN by Alexandra Ivy/Laura Wright
DRAGON KING by Donna Grant
PURE WICKED by Shayla Black
HARD AS STEEL by Laura Kaye
STROKE OF MIDNIGHT by Lara Adrian
ALL HALLOWS EVE by Heather Graham
KISS THE FLAME by Christopher Rice
DARING HER LOVE by Melissa Foster
TEASED by Rebecca Zanetti
THE PROMISE OF SURRENDER by Liliana Hart

COLLECTION THREE
HIDDEN INK by Carrie Ann Ryan
BLOOD ON THE BAYOU by Heather Graham
SEARCHING FOR MINE by Jennifer Probst
DANCE OF DESIRE by Christopher Rice
ROUGH RHYTHM by Tessa Bailey
DEVOTED by Lexi Blake
Z by Larissa Ione
FALLING UNDER YOU by Laurelin Paige
EASY FOR KEEPS by Kristen Proby
UNCHAINED by Elisabeth Naughton
HARD TO SERVE by Laura Kaye
DRAGON FEVER by Donna Grant
KAYDEN/SIMON by Alexandra Ivy/Laura Wright
STRUNG UP by Lorelei James
MIDNIGHT UNTAMED by Lara Adrian
TRICKED by Rebecca Zanetti
DIRTY WICKED by Shayla Black
THE ONLY ONE by Lauren Blakely
SWEET SURRENDER by Liliana Hart

COLLECTION FOUR
ROCK CHICK REAWAKENING by Kristen Ashley
ADORING INK by Carrie Ann Ryan
SWEET RIVALRY by K. Bromberg
SHADE'S LADY by Joanna Wylde
RAZR by Larissa Ione
ARRANGED by Lexi Blake
TANGLED by Rebecca Zanetti
HOLD ME by J. Kenner
SOMEHOW, SOME WAY by Jennifer Probst
TOO CLOSE TO CALL by Tessa Bailey
HUNTED by Elisabeth Naughton
EYES ON YOU by Laura Kaye
BLADE by Alexandra Ivy/Laura Wright
DRAGON BURN by Donna Grant
TRIPPED OUT by Lorelei James

About Jill Shalvis

New York Times and *USA Today* bestselling author Jill Shalvis writes warm, funny, sexy contemporary romances and women's fiction. An Amazon, BN & iBooks bestseller, she's also a two-time RITA winner and has more than 10 million copies of her books sold worldwide.

Jill lives with her family in a small town in the Sierras full of quirky characters (Any resemblance to the quirky characters in her books is mostly coincidental). She does most of her writing on her deck surrounded by more animals than humans. Which is quite astonishing considering she's a city girl who was plucked from the wilds of L.A. to the wilds of the Sierra's. Most of her books come from a combination of hard work, cookies, and hot guy pics, and not necessarily in that order.

Wrapped Up in You
A Heartbreaker Bay Novel
By Jill Shalvis
Coming September 24, 2019

Don't miss the newest book in my New York Times
Bestselling Heartbreaker Bay series

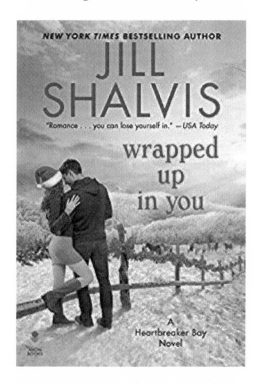

It's love. Trust me.

After a lifetime on the move, Ivy Snow is an expert in all things temporary—schools, friends, and way too many Mr. Wrongs. Now that she owns a successful taco truck in San Francisco and an apartment to call home, Ivy's reinvented life is on solid ground. And she's guarded against anything that can rock it. Like the realities of a past she's worked hard to cover up. And especially Kel O'Donnell.

Too hot not to set off alarms, he screams temporary. If only his whispers weren't so delightfully naughty and irresistible.

Kel, an Idaho sheriff and ranch owner, is on vacay, but Ivy's a spicy reason to give his short-terms plans a second thought. Best of all, she's a tonic for his untrusting heart, burned once and still in repair. But when Ivy's past intrudes on a perfect romance, Kel fears that everything she's told him has been a perfect lie. Now, if only Ivy's willing to share, Kel will fight for a *true* love story.

Excerpt:

Kel O'Donnell stood there in front of The Taco Truck, starving and aching like a son-of-a-bitch. Pushing his body on a five mile full out run hadn't been the smartest of ideas after what he'd been through. But his more immediate problem was that if he didn't get food and fast, his stomach was going to eat itself.

The woman inside the truck looked to him for his order. "And you?" she asked, her voice slightly amused, as if life wasn't to be taken too seriously, especially while ordering tacos.

But he was taking this very seriously, as his hunger felt soul deep. "What do you suggest?"

This caused twin groans from his cousin Caleb and their longtime friend Jake, which Kel ignored.

Not his server though. She quirked a single brow, the small gesture making him feel more than he had in months. Certainly since his life had detonated several months ago when he'd chased after a suspect on foot, only to be hit by the getaway car, getting himself punted a good fifteen feet into the air. That had hurt. But what had hurt more was his perp turning out to be a dirty cop. And not any dirty cop, but a long time friend, which had nearly cost him life and career.

But hell, at least neither were on the line this time. It was just a pretty woman giving him some cute, sexy 'tude while waiting on him to decide between an avocado and bacon tacos, or spicy green eggs and ham tacos.

"You're going to have to excuse my dumbass cousin, Ivy," Caleb said. "Kel hasn't lived in San Francisco for a long time and doesn't know that you've got the best food truck in all of Cow Hollow. Hell, in the whole bay area."

"It's true," Jake said and nudged Kel, and with Jake in the wheelchair, he got the nudge right in the back of the knee and just about went down.

"Everything on the menu," Jake said, "and I do mean everything is gold. Trust me, it'll melt in your mouth and make you want to drop to your knees and beg Ivy here to marry you."

Ivy sent Jake the sweetest smile Kel had ever seen. Then those compelling eyes were back on him, the sweet completely gone. She leaned out her serving window a little bit, bracing her weight on her elbows. Her hair was the color of fire, a stunning pile of red held back by an elf headband, which left a few strands falling around her face, framing it. Her apron read: I don't wanna taco 'bout it. "What do I suggest?" she repeated.

"Yeah." Just looking at her, he could feel himself relax for the first time in … way too long. Something about her did that to him. Instant chemistry. He hadn't felt it often in his life and it always ended up a train wreck, so why the hell he felt relaxed, he had no idea. But it had him flashing another smile. "How about you pick for me."

Her lips quirked at that. "Fair warning -- I like things hot."

"I love things hot," he said.

Jake just grinned. "Aw man, she's gonna eat you up and spit you out. I'm so happy."

"Shh," Caleb said. "I don't want to miss him getting his ass handed to him."

Ivy just cocked her head at Kel. "Think you can handle the heat?"

"Oh yeah."

"Five minutes." And she shut the window on them.

They moved to one of the two picnic tables at the entrance to the courtyard in front of them, where they sat to wait for their food. Caleb looked at Kel and shook his head. "Man, as much as I enjoy seeing you get your ego squashed, I feel duty bound to warn you. Whatever's making you smile, it's never going to happen. Ivy's not the girl you have fun with and walk away from. And plus, she hates cops."

"Agreed," Jake said. "You've got a better shot at stealing Sadie away from Caleb. And good luck with that. Your cousin's woman is batshit crazy over him, God knows why."

Caleb just smiled, apparently not feeling the need to defend his relationship.

Kel was happy for him. Very happy. Caleb hadn't given his heart away ... ever. And for good reasons, which Kel had hated for him. "About time you found someone who deserves you."

Caleb was quiet a moment. "I like having you here," he said, kind enough to leave out the tone of recrimination. It'd been a long time, too long, which had been all Kel's doing. He'd spent the first ten years of his life here in the city, he and his sister and his parents. They'd lived next door to his aunt and her kids, including Caleb. Kel hadn't realized at the time, but they'd all been poor as dirt, even though his parents had always managed to make it seem like they'd had everything they'd needed.

Then his mom had destroyed that happy illusion with a single, shattering mistake, creating a huge rift none of them had recovered from. Two years later had come yet another blow. His dad had died, and Kel and his older sister Remy had gone to Idaho to be raised by their grandparents.

It'd sucked.

"You see Remy yet?" Caleb asked.

Kel's sister had moved back here to San Francisco after getting married last year. And no, he hadn't seen her yet. And yes, he was stalling.

"Okay ... how about your mom?" Caleb asked.

Kel slid him a look.

Caleb raised his hands. "Hey, just asking."

"Uh huh. Do you ask all your employees such personal questions?"

"No, just my brother."

"I'm your cousin."

"You're my brother," Caleb said with meaning.

Kel sighed and looked over at Jake.

Jake shrugged. "He likes to adjust facts to suit him. But you knew that already."

Ivy came out of the truck with three baskets. She served Jake first, then Caleb, and finally Kel. She handed him his basket and stood there at his side, a tiny pixie of a woman in that sassy apron, elf headband, and painted on jeans faded to a buttery softness. Her boots were serious and kickass, and because he was a very sick man, they turned him on.

Since she was clearly going nowhere until he tried her food, he took a bite of what looked like the most amazing breakfast taco he'd ever seen and ... almost died. Spicy was an understatement. Holy hell hot was an understatement. But it was also the best thing he'd ever tasted, even if his tongue was numb.

Ivy smiled at him. "Still think you can handle the heat?"

Jake and Caleb were doubled over laughing, the asses. "I'm not a cop," he managed to wheeze, holding her gaze while he took another bite. And another. No doubt, he was going to eat her food the entire three weeks he was here. If he lived that long.

"He's a sheriff and ranch owner in Idaho," Caleb said. "So ... kind of a cop."

"Also kind of a cowboy," Jake added ever so helpfully.

Kel rolled his still watering eyes. His grandparents had left him and Remy their ranch, which he oversaw, but had employees handling the day to day operations since his day job was more like a 24/7 job. "I'm just a guy on vacay," he croaked out. The more accurate term would have been assigned slash medical leave, but hell if he was going to share that. Or the fact that his still healing broken ribs ached like a bitch, as did the deep bone bruising he'd suffered down the entire right side of his body from being pitched into the air by a moving vehicle.

Caleb snorted. "You don't do vacay. As evidenced by the fact you agreed to work for me for the entire two weeks you're here. I needed him," he said to Ivy. "He's got serious skills. He's going to manage security on several large projects, including my most recently acquired building, the one being renovated into condos." He looked at Kel. "Ivy's going to buy one with her brother, who's an antiquities specialist. It's a great investment," he said like a proud parent, even though at thirty-two, he couldn't have been more than five years or so older than Ivy.

"Actually, it might just be me investing," Ivy said. "Brandon just got into a deal on the east coast I was telling you about."

"The auction house job."

"Yes, and it's going to keep him busy for a while, so..." She shrugged. "I told him I'd go after this myself."

"That's too bad," Caleb said. "Was looking forward to meeting him."

Kel stopped chewing because something in Ivy's tone had just set off his bullshit radar. She was either lying or stretching the truth, but his eyes were still watering and his throat was burning or he might've joined the conversation.

Ivy reached out as if to take away his basket, but he held firm to it and kept eating. He was starting to sweat and he couldn't feel his lips, but he also couldn't get enough.

"Okay, Cowboy, it's your funeral," she said, and he couldn't tell if she was impressed or horrified.

A few more people were milling around her truck now, and she eyed her watch.

"They start lining up earlier every day," Caleb said.

"Hey, Ivy," one of the guys who was waiting called out. "The fuzz! They're coming around the corner!"

"Crap!" Ivy ran towards her truck, yelling to the people standing in line, "I'll be back in ten minutes. If you wait and save my spot, I'll give you a discount!" And then she slapped the window and door closed and roared off down the street.

A minute later a cop drove by slowly, but didn't stop. When he was gone, the group of people who'd been lining up for tacos stepped into the empty parking spot Ivy had left.

Not ten seconds later, a car came along and honked at the people standing in the spot. "Get out of my way," the driver yelled.

No one budged.

The car window lowered and a hand emerged, flipping everyone the bird.

This didn't make anyone move either, and finally the guy swore and drove off in a huff.

"What the hell?" Kel asked.

"She's not supposed to be on the street before seven," Jake said.

"I'm working on getting her a city permit," Caleb said. "They're extremely hard to get."

Kel was boggled. "But … those people are blocking the street. They could get a ticket."

"Thought you weren't a cop," Caleb said, looking amused.

Kel shook his head and went back to his tacos, and for a guy who believed in the law, when the incredible burst of flavors once again hit his tongue, he thought maybe he could understand the flagrant disregard of it in this one case.

On behalf of 1001 Dark Nights,

Liz Berry and M.J. Rose would like to thank ~

Steve Berry
Doug Scofield
Kim Guidroz
Jillian Stein
InkSlinger PR
Dan Slater
Asha Hossain
Chris Graham
Chelle Olson
Jessica Johns
Dylan Stockton
Richard Blake
and Simon Lipskar

Made in the USA
Middletown, DE
03 November 2019